Manifesto for the Dead

Manifesto for the Dead

by

Domenic Stansberry

THE PERMANENT PRESS
SAG HARBOR, NY 11963

Library of Congress Cataloging-in-Publication Data

Stansberry, Domenic
Manifesto for the Dead / by Domenic Stansberry
p. cm.
ISBN 1-57962-059-0
I. Thompson, Jim, 1906-1977 Fiction. I. Title.
PS3569.T3335M36 2000
813'.54--dc21 99-30775
CIP

THE PERMANENT PRESS
4170 Noyac Road
Sag Harbor, NY 11963

ONE

THIS WAS THE END. The final trap. The last flimflam. And for Jim Thompson, this ending—this long plunge into the sweet nothing—was set in motion on the day he first met Billy Miracle, at the Musso & Frank Grill, down on Hollywood Boulevard.

It was 1971, and Thompson came to Musso's almost every afternoon. He was a crime writer, a novelist and scriptwriter who'd first seen Hollywood almost thirty years before. Now he was sixty-four years old, with flame white hair and dark, hooded eyes. He leaned among the other regulars at the bar, hearing little whispers of infinity. The whispering rose from the bottom of his glass, or seemed to, but the voice was his own.

You're at bottom of the pit, Jimmy. No call's coming and even your wife won't fuck you. I can smell you decomposing.

Thompson glanced around Musso's. It was a fashionable gutter joint, with dark walls and red booths and boozy air that smelled of cigarettes and chicken-fried steak. The place had a mixed clientele. Hollywood people fresh off the studio lots. Neighborhood regulars. Also writers and actors who came to hustle something and kept coming, night after night. Sooner or later, they all ended up at the bar.

Behind that bar a mirror reflected your image back to you, so everyone seemed to linger in two worlds at once: the dark, murky world of the present; and that other world just beyond, shimmering in the illusive clarity of the mirror. It was to that other world everyone was trying to go, with their highballs and their straight shots and their hustles and their schemes.

Thompson was looking into that mirror when Billy Miracle appeared, sidling up from out of the crowd. "I'm a fan," Miracle said. "I've read every one of your goddamn books."

Miracle was in his late forties, sliding towards fifty. He wore a white sport coat, a black shirt beneath it. He was dark-skinned and not bad-looking, with short, dark hair and watery brown eyes that had a bit of a glint to them. He had a hawkish nose and a quick smile. He was the kind of guy you wanted to like when you talked to him, but later, you wondered what price you might have to pay.

"Come on," Miracle said. His voice was soft like linen, his breath smelled of garlic. "Let me buy you a drink."

Thompson hesitated, but not long enough. "All right," he said. "That would be swell."

•

Miracle's real name was Abe Syncowitz. Rumor said he was hooked up with the Jewish mob, and somehow he'd used that muscle to get himself into the picture business. He'd made a half-dozen shoot 'em ups, drive-in stuff mostly, with titles like *Bullet in the Brain* and *The End of Time.* The stories involved small-time hoods who suddenly found themselves stumbling among the rich and glamorous, and the movies always ended in a wash of blood.

Though the films had made money, Miracle had a bad reputation. His head was full of snow. He schemed crazy schemes. Worse, Miracle was in debt big time to the Vegas mobster who'd bankrolled his last film. And that debt was coming due.

How much of this was true, Thompson had no idea.

Until now, he'd only seen the man from a distance. All he knew for certain was Miracle's studio had pulled the plug, and the producer had been in and out of Musso's these last few weeks, trying to work a new angle.

It seemed Miracle had hooked himself up with a fading star named Michele Haze. Haze was Jack Lombard's old girl, and Lombard—as everybody knew—was the green light man for half the pictures in town. Lombard and Haze had been an item for years, but they were finished now. So Billy Miracle had stepped in. He was shopping some kind of screenplay that featured her in the main role.

"A love triangle. Set right here in Los Angeles."

"A love triangle?"

"That's right. And you know how that type of thing ends, don't you?"

"How?"

They regarded themselves in the looking glass, the haggard old writer and the producer on the make. Meanwhile, behind them in the shadows—in the red booths under the dim light—others moved and mingled, speaking in voices that were voluptuous, full of intention.

"Everyone gets fucked, that's how. Anyway, I've got a proposal for you."

"What's that?"

"The screenplay—I think it might be easier to sell if it was part of a package."

"I'm not sure."

"A book. What I need, is somebody to write a novel based on the screenplay. Then, I'm thinking, if we have book interest, we can get movie interest too."

It was a screwball scheme, but time was running out. Alberta, Thompson's wife, had gone this afternoon to look at a place more in their budget, a rummy little joint on the hill behind Graumann's Chinese. She didn't want to move, though, and neither did he.

"I'd be interested."

Miracle seemed not to hear. Thompson guessed what the other man was doing. Laying out the bait. Tugging the string through the water. Waiting for the fish to lunge hard at the hook. Thompson raised his glass to his lips. He swirled the whiskey in his mouth, as if anesthetizing his upper lip. Then he went ahead and bit.

"The book. I could do that."

They regarded one another once again in the mirror. Miracle's eyes had grown fierce. "I don't want the book and the movie to tell the same story. You see the main action of the movie involves this love triangle, here in Los Angeles. But the killer's from Texas, and the movie tells his story too. Back and forth. A story in Texas, a story here. When the two come together . . . ." Miracle turned from the mirror now and faced Thompson directly. He looked him in the eyes. "I want your book to tell the story of the killer. The guy in Texas. He's your job."

"Do you have any money? An advance?"

"You have to be a son of a bitch in this business. Look at the streets and you see. Pimps. Whores. Robbers and thieves. You forget the basics, you're on the asphalt. That's the way life is."

Thompson had heard this kind of talk before. It was the sort of rant producers went into when you brought up the subject of money. In the face of it, he fell quiet. He swilled the whiskey around the bottom of his glass, knocked it down, stared at the ice.

Miracle went on. "They're ruthless out there. They'll cut your throat. Take your wallet. Fuck your mother."

Miracle slapped his glass onto the countertop, motioned to the bartender for another round.

"Look at Lombard. How do you think he got where he is? He screwed you to the wall too, didn't he?"

Thompson said nothing. He didn't want to talk about Lombard.

"Well, you're not the only one who's been shut out. Ever since he's hooked up with that new girl of his, The Young Lovely, no one can get through to him anymore. She has her fingers on everything. You know how it goes. The Young Lovely—she's got his balls wrapped up in her skirt."

"Can I see the screenplay? If the book's based on the movie—then, it might help."

"Just start writing. Give me a few pages. "Miracle reached over and gave him a pat on the back. "Don't worry, Jimbo. You and me, we're simpatico. Peas from a pod."

Thompson didn't like the sound of this deal, but he didn't know what else to do. It was the same old business, the hangman's trap, damned either way you dangle. Then the bartender slid them each a new drink. The whiskey put a pleasant haze over the mirror. Everyone seemed to be moving in a kind of warm, amber fluid.

"What do you think Lombard would do if the positions were reversed?"

"What do you mean?"

"You know, if that starlet—The Young Lovely—if she was in *his* way. So that he couldn't get to the people he needed."

Thompson thought about it, but the truth was he could not imagine Lombard in such a position.

"So what do you think he'd do?"

"Bury her," Thompson said at last.

"That's right. He'd just lay her right into the ground." Miracle laughed. It was an unpleasant laugh, of a kind he'd also heard before. In the old days, back when he'd worked as a writer at the *Police Gazette.* On the set of *The Getaway,* when he'd been writing dialogue for Steve McQueen. In the editorial offices at Lion Books and at Random House. Men laughing over corpses, imaginary or otherwise. From the way they laughed, you would think they were murderers themselves. Most of them weren't (or if they were, they kept it under wraps). They were family men. They had wives at home. Yards with a picket fence. A daughter who threw her arms around daddy's neck when he walked through the door.

Thompson took another swallow and pretty soon Miracle slipped away, folding back into the crowd, working other angles, shaking other hands. Thompson regarded his own image in the mirror, and for a second there was a clarity about it, sitting there among all those others, and he wondered if maybe this time things would be different. If maybe there was another world on the other side of that mirror, and he would somehow slip through at last. Then he slugged down the rest of his drink and walked out onto the streets.

Outside it was the same dirty business as always. If you believed the stories, Hollywood Boulevard had been quite the stroll once upon a while. The Great White Way. Flooded with light. The people all but shimmering as they promenaded down the avenue. Maybe so, but now there was not much open but the bars and the skin joints. He walked past the flesh hustlers, turned the corner at Whitely, up the hill toward the Ardmore. He went through the lobby with its globes of yellow light and into the elevator. He stepped into his apartment, looking for Alberta to tell her about his new job.

He found her in the bedroom, by the closet, with her blouse undone. She stood in her skirt and her bra, regarding her aging self in the vanity. She was closing in on sixty, but she looked pretty good. His wife still had her shape. When she looked at him the way she did just now, with those eyes of hers, all green ice and blazing light, he felt her glance like a blow in the chest.

"You asked him how much, honey? You did that, didn't you?"

"Sure."

"Well, how much?"

"We're still negotiating."

"In other words, you're going to get screwed again." Then she turned away from him, buttoning up her blouse, and he felt his heart—which had risen a moment, fluttering like a canary—plummet into his bowels.

TWO

THE THOMPSONS' PENTHOUSE apartment was on the top floor of the Hollywood Ardmore, only a few blocks from the strip, but it was a world away. The walls were white, the carpets plush. There were wall-to-wall windows in the living room, and sliding doors that opened onto the balcony. In the evenings you could stand out on that balcony, twelve stories up, and look towards Santa Monica and the ocean and all the hazy lights in-between.

It should have been a pleasant enough place to work but he could not get anything done.

The reason was Alberta. She stood in front of him now in her green shift and matching pumps. She was a fierce woman, with her silver hair and her hands on her waist and her body that still smelled to him like the honey-suckle vines curling over his mother's porch.

"No matter how much that producer offers, we have to be out of here by the end of the month. Our lease is up."

"We can renew it."

"It's too late. I made the arrangements for the place on Hillcrest. The one I told you about."

"It's never too late," he said, though he knew better than to believe such nonsense. He strolled over and tried to give her a kiss. She raised a finger between his lips and her own.

"You've been drinking."

"Just a little."

"Last night. The night before. And now this after-noon. You remember what the doctor said."

Thompson remembered well enough. If he didn't

take better care of himself, then soon, well, he wouldn't have to worry about anything at all. He could just forget everything. No worries, no cares. Hang around in a pine box, dressed in his good suit. Take it easy for so long as he liked.

Alberta went on talking. Thompson glanced out the window at the flatlands of the Los Angeles Basin. He felt himself descending. Down there once again into the land of hard light and black shadows.

"Why?" said Alberta.

He had not been listening, but he'd heard the anger in her voice, and saw her expression, and recognized in it the old dilemma, the old devil's mix, suspicion and desire, hate and love, all that stuff—soft flesh, hard bone, cock and cunt. It had been there ever since he'd first put his hand up her skirt, a million years ago, maybe two million, and looked into her simmering eyes.

"Goddamn it, Jim. Why don't you pull your head out of the casket and smell the roses." She wheeled away, off into the bedroom.

If he wanted to get any work done, he would have to check himself a room somewhere. In a transient hotel, a roadside inn, anything he could afford. He'd done the same in the past, when they were younger and lived in two-bit squalor, and he would do so again now.

Trouble was, he needed money even for that.

•

He went to the kitchen and picked up the phone. Quietly, hoping Alberta would not hear, he dialed his sister in La Jolla. He told her his problem.

"All right, Jim," Franny said.

The sound of his sister's voice reminded him of his mother. Of all the little fly-by-nowhere joints they'd lived in as kids. It was the sound of the wind leaking through the wooden boards of a shack at the edge of some town no one wanted to live in anymore. Of Anadarko, Oklahoma, where he was born.

"You and Alberta fighting again?"

"No."

"Whatever you say. Bill and I are leaving tomorrow."

"Where to?"

"Lincoln."

They were always going to Nebraska, Franny and Bill. They had relatives there, friends from the old days. People with thin faces and checkered shirts who'd made their money in hogs and corn.

"How long you be gone?"

"Couple weeks. I'll put a check in the mail to you before I go, Jim. If that'll help."

"Thanks, Sis."

"You're welcome to stay here, at our place."

"No." He was tempted, though. His sister's place was just a few blocks from the ocean.

"While we're in Lincoln, you want me to look up Lucille?"

"Lucille?"

Thompson played it dumb, but he knew damn well who she meant. Lussie Jones. Lucille, really, though no one called her that except other women, sometimes, or those who did not know her well. They'd lain together on the side of a hill once, fingers touching. Back in some other century, it seemed. The night had been grubby with humidity, the sky black, full of stars.

His sister waited on the other end. She knew the story. He had told her once, sloshed to the gills.

"Well, no, I don't think so," he said.

Later, as if in a dream—standing over an open grave

in the Hollywood Hills—Thompson would think back on this moment and wonder if there was anything he could have done to change what was to happen. If he had not called his sister, for instance. If he had stayed with Alberta in the Ardmore. Or turned down Billy Miracle.

Or if instead, everything that had happened was part of the fabric of things, the warp and the woof, no matter his actions, and there was nothing he could do.

Either way, Thompson got off the phone. When he turned, there stood Alberta, arms akimbo, with that green blaze in her eyes. If she had heard him mention the other woman's name, he didn't know, and he wasn't about to ask.

THREE

HIS SISTER SENT THE MONEY. Thompson checked himself a room in the Aztec Hotel, just off Sunset, in a neighborhood of small hotels and whitewashed bungalows. The Aztec itself was three stories high. A red brick affair, with a sunbeaten awning hanging over the main entry. On the other side of that entry, a clerk worked the lobby desk.

Thompson paid the clerk—a snide, snarly, drugged-up kid in a red jacket. Then he clomped upstairs to his room.

He hadn't brought much with him. A change of clothes. A bottle of Jack. His Hermes portable. Also, an old six-shooter that had belonged to his father: an 1886 Retriever. The Retriever was an antique of sorts—a 45 caliper Army issue renowned for its faulty firing mechanism. Thompson brought it along for luck.

He thought of the young clerk who had checked him in.Ugly kid.Back when he was an ugly kid himself, Thompson had worked in an hotel too. His father had dragged the family down south to Fort Worth on a wildcatting scheme, but the scheme had gone sour.

He'd been writing back then as well, hiding his pages under the hotel blotter. He was plagued by erections, steaming up out of nowhere (a problem that had never left him, not completely, not even as an old man, lost in a muddle of words and drink). As a bell clerk, in those days, it had been his job to provide certain services. That meant knocking on brothel doors, bringing back a girl, some bootleg, maybe, or loco weed from the barrios of Dallas.

On occasion the hotel guests invited him to the party. Usually he ended up alone. Roaming the corridors impulsively. It was a trait with him, that impulsiveness, especially when drinking. He entered doors without knocking.

Sorry, he'd whisper. Just delivering towels. Hotel business.

He was no longer that green kid, but in some ways not much had changed. He was still scribbling. Except now he had a different angle; that of an old man sitting at a hotel window, a cigarette in his hand, a half-empty bottle on the table, an incessant cough, blood in his spittle. A man who in the mirror looked a decade older than he was. Raccoon eyes. Skin like the bark on some tree gone to rot.

Oh, well. Miracle, at least, had given him a title.

MANIFESTO FOR THE DEAD

I was standing on the edge of one of those nowhere little Texas towns where the whole world looks like it's been painted black and white. On the road ahead, prairie and more prairie, and it was the same thing back the other direction. It had been almost an hour since the last car went by.

There's a lesson in this, boy.

It was the voice again. Pops. He'd been with me since I could remember. Hardly a good word to say.

If only you'd listen, maybe you'd learn a thing or two.

I was about ready to snap, I guess, between dealing with Pops in my head and standing out there in all that Texas nothing. Then a car appeared on the horizon. It approached slow, coming up out of the heat and the haze. I put my thumb out, and its wheels churned dust all over hell.

A woman motioned me in. She had wide, baby doll eyes, and lips painted the color of a barn door. She smiled and fixed her eyes on mine. I felt something twist inside.

You're a sap, boy, said Pops. *Nothing but a goddamn sap.*

FOUR

IN THE MORNING, ALBERTA CALLED. Her voice was pleasant and bright, as if there were nothing wrong between them. He could picture her twelve stories up in the Ardmore, sitting there cross-legged on the couch in her Bermuda shorts and sleeveless blouse.

"I need you at the Hillcrest Arms this afternoon," she said. "The old tenant has cleared out—and a man from the gas company will be along to adjust the pilot."

"Aren't we jumping the gun?"

"And oh. That producer called. Mr. Billy Miracle."

"What did he want?"

"To meet with you. I told him you were going to be at the Hillcrest apartment. I gave him the address."

"No." Thompson didn't like Miracle knowing his business.

"Don't worry. Mr. Miracle said it would be better if you courier over some pages in advance. Then meet him down at Musso's."

Thompson had more to say, but Alberta did not give him a chance. Her voice was so cheerful, he dared not argue. Any objections and misgivings, odd forebodings rising up out of his gut, any of this, he left unsaid.

•

That afternoon Thompson headed for the apartment on Hillcrest, working his way though the back streets of Hollywood. The Hillcrest Arms was an apartment building in the Moroccan style, brooding over a sloping little park with a banyan tree. The surrounding neighborhood was strewn with old wrecks. A cop car rolled by, a cruiser on patrol, and Thompson caught a glimpse of the two dicks inside. They were the usual buzzards, grim, bored, squinting through the windshield in their blue suits.

Thompson pushed through the doors and walked down the darkened hall until he reached the apartment Alberta had reserved for them. The place was as bad as he feared: a narrow one bedroom, gray walls, green carpet. For no reason at all, he thought of Lussie Jones. Maybe it was because his sister had mentioned her just a few days ago. Or because places like this, even in their emptiness, were musty with the smell of desire.

He looked down at his crotch. It had come undone, and the sight of himself—undone like that—aroused him. As he reached down to do up the buttons, the door buzzer went off.

Thompson stepped out into the hall. At the end of the corridor, on the other side of the glass entry, stood a young man. It took the young man another instant to realize the door was unlocked, then he pulled the handle. Thompson watched him come. A thin man, lean and gawky. He knifed through the shadows with a nervous, stuttering gait.

"Mr. Wicks?"

Thompson pinned it right away. The Okie accent. Not too different from his own. Nasal and slow and a little hesitant, the sound of a motor sputtering through the corn.

"You with the utility company?"

"I'm looking for a man named Wicks. Sydney Wicks."

"Then you got the wrong place."

"This is number 22, ain't it? I can see right here. Come on, don't pull my trousers."

"Maybe you got your orders mixed?"

"Huh?"

"We got a pilot light needs firing."

Thompson stepped into the apartment, and the young man followed. They regarded one another in the light. The Okie was about thirty. He had blonde hair, cut short, and piercing blue eyes that were so innocent as to be menacing, and a stance that was like that of an adolescent boy just come into manhood. He clutched and unclutched his hand, stared at Thompson fiercely, then looked around the room in a confused manner. The expression on his face said there was something askew—as if Thompson were not the person he'd expected him to be.

The Okie held a piece of paper in one hand, his keys in the other. He wore a gray, uniform-style shirt, but there was no name on it. His face was oily and haggard.

Outside, an old Cadillac stood parked under the banyan tree. It hadn't been there a few minutes before.

"You're with the utility company, that right?"

The man ran a hand through his yellow hair. "Come on, Wicks. Let's see the money."

"I told you, my name's not Wicks."

Thompson heard the fear in his own voice, and felt the situation about to go wrong. The stranger's eyes widened. He slapped his keys on the mantle and thrust the paper at Thompson.

"This is where I was told to come, with the delivery."

Thompson examined the paper. On one side, written in a tall, looping hand, was the Hillcrest address. On the other side, though, was a different address all together.

"Look." Thompson tried to show him the other address.

The Okie was sweating, his eyes wide and nervous. He ran his fingers once again through all that blonde bristle. "Fuck," he said. Then he glanced toward the window. "Jesus fuck."

Thompson saw what the Okie had seen. The cop car glimmering in the heat, returning from the other direction. In an instant, the Okie was out in the hallway, headed for the rear of the building. Thompson followed. The back door banged shut, and the Okie was gone. Thompson turned. Through the glass doors at the front entry, he caught the cruiser pause at the stop sign, then take the corner. The dicks looked in no particular hurry. Everything was routine.

Thompson went back to the apartment. His hands shook. He took a drink from the little flask he carried in his pocket. As he stood there, toying with the addresses on the paper, he spotted a dull glint on the mantle.

The son of a bitch had forgotten his keys.

Outside, Thompson circled the block, but there was no one. The Okie had vanished. He looked for a utility van, or a service truck, but there was nothing like that on the streets. Only the Cadillac, over there, under the banyan tree.

Despite himself, he thumbed through the keys on the Okie's ring. One of them, he thought, might be a fit.

Overhead, the palms rustled in the hot wind. They looked like tall women with idiot hairdos, swaying in the heat. Thompson could hear the traffic on Franklin, the persistent hum of Los Angeles that seemed to hold within itself the silence of the desert.

He told himself to stay away, but he went over to the banyan tree. Underneath it, the Cadillac stood covered with dust, as if it had just been driven on a long journey. He walked around to the back of the car, the key still in his hands.

What he did next, he had a hard time explaining to himself. Maybe I guessed, he told himself later. Maybe

I already knew, deep down, what was inside that trunk. The Okie's slouch told me, the smell of his skin, the nervousness in his eyes. Or maybe it was just the old nosiness. I just wanted to see if the key would turn the lock.

The key turned. A young woman lay before him. Her eyes were milky, and she was bruised about the throat.

In that moment, it seemed, Thomson could hear all the voices in the desert that was the great city of Los Angeles. He could hear them in the whispering of God's littlest creatures, the tiniest flies, invisible maggots, as they set busily to their work.

FIVE

THOMPSON CLOSED THE TRUNK, but the girl's image stayed with him. A brunette, with an oval face, all black and blue. Someone had draped a sheet over her body, but haphazardly, so she resembled a fitful sleeper who'd thrown off her covers. Only there was something wrong about her neck, and about her legs, too, the way they angled and twisted into the wheel well.

She'd been beaten badly, and strangled about the neck.

Behind her, in the back of the car's huge trunk, there'd been a brand new shovel. Someone had meant to bury her, maybe. The girl had not been dead long. There was still color in her cheeks, and her body had not yet begun to stink.

Thompson stood with his palms flat against the trunk. The time to go was now, but he didn't. The street was empty. The nearby porches, the gray windows and overhanging balconies—they were all flooded with white light. He raised his hand to brush away the heat, then he heard a car rushing down Hillcrest Avenue from the hills above the Hollywood Bowl. He could have behaved differently—he could have flagged the car down, maybe, called the police—but standing there, the key in his hand, he was overcome with an inexplicable guilt, as if he were the one responsible for the girl's death. It was the guilt one feels in a dream, moving down corridors to escape punishment for some half-remembered crime. The car was closer now, approaching the corner, and he did not have time to make it into the building without being seen. So he climbed into the Cadillac. (It was the alcohol, he would think later, or the sun in his eyes, the old jumpiness, a perpetual flaw, that made him leap the way he did.) He sat behind the wheel and turned his face as the car went by.

Go to the cops, he told himself. But that would mean explaining everything. Not just the Okie, but how he himself had taken the man's keys, popped the trunk.

My fingerprints are all over the car, he thought. The cops will hold me on suspicion.

They could detain him forty-eight hours without cause, he knew—and without liquor. The thought made him twitch. He had been through withdrawal before. The idea of going through the terrors while under interrogation, in a cell, in a dark room. . .

His mind searched around for an alternative. . . what could be done. . . with the girl. . . the car. . .

He took the flask from his pocket, felt the whiskey burn in his gut. A feeling of strength, the old rush, the sidewalk shimmering. Then the tremor came again, a hard shiver—a sanitarium shiver almost, as if the fabric of the world were tearing apart, the light disintegrating into dark—and he had to take another drink. Then he heard another car rolling down Hillcrest, and the panic moved him to action. He had to get out of here. He turned the key. The ignition fired.

He pulled onto Franklin, then urged the Cadillac slowly across Highland Avenue, not far from the Ardmore.

What now?

He was implicating himself, he knew, worse with every action. He had to get rid of the Cadillac. Out in the desert, far away. But then how would he get back? And how would he explain where he'd been?

He braked at a stop sign. A car came up from behind. He took a hard left, away from the car, into the

Hollywood Hills, and he realized suddenly what he was going to do.

He drove past the old Iago Hotel, climbing up a short, steep grade to the east side of Whitely Terrace, following it until the houses ran out and the asphalt became gravel. Then he killed the engine, easing the Caddy up close to a cyclone fence that ran along the ridge.

The Hollywood Freeway was at the bottom of that ridge, rushing through the canyon below. This spot was not exactly isolated, but it was out of sight, a patch of stone and dirt hidden from the plate glass windows above and the freeway below by a stand of eucalyptus grown out of control. It might be a few days before anyone noticed the car. Then he reached into the back and grabbed a red sweater that lay on the seat. A fine, soft material. Cashmere, he guessed, property of the deceased.

The sweater carried the smell of perfume and the odor of sweat, musky and faint, and that odor seemed to fill the car as he clutched the fabric between his hands. He used the sweater as a rag, wiping his prints from anything he had touched. He worked hurriedly, nervously, and when he finished, he left the keys in the ignition. Maybe someone would steal the goddamn car, he thought, and take the whole nightmare off my hands.

He bundled the sweater into a paper bag and headed down the hill. His prints might be on the fabric, and he needed to get rid of it someplace else, away from the scene.

Not far ahead, there was a break in the cyclone fence. A ragged little path ran into the brush nearby. Further down he could see a dirt road of some sort, on the slope above the freeway. The city had been doing some trench work there, but the job seemed to have been abandoned. It was the way things were these days, half finished jobs everywhere. The murderer had intended to bury the girl, but it wasn't going to happen now. Not unless I do it myself, and his heart fluttered horribly. I could finish the job tonight, roll her into the trench, be done with it. He reached for his flask and pushed the thought away. He'd gotten himself too involved with this already. Besides, he was an old man and didn't have the strength for wrestling with a dead woman in the Hollywood Hills.

SIX

BACK ON THE BOULEVARD, Thompson went into Musso's and had himself the pork chop special and a pair of drinks. He waited for Billy Miracle. All the while, the sweater sat inside the bag on the seat beside him. It gave off a sweet, womanly smell. He'd been unable to get rid of it, out there in the broad daylight.

Thompson finished his set-up, then ordered another.

Finally, Miracle showed. The producer didn't come directly to Thompson, though. He leaned his head into a booth, talking to a woman there.

If Thompson were not still shaking from what had happened on the hill, he might have recognized the woman a beat sooner. Then he knew. It was the movie star, Michele Haze, Lombard's old flame. An arresting woman in her early forties, Haze was a platinum blonde with pale features and dark eyes. At the moment, she sat in a sultry, slump-shouldered way, enshrouded in blue smoke.

Miracle held a hand on her shoulder, then he let loose and came toward Thompson, carrying with him the opening pages Thompson had sent by courier.

"Meetings, meetings. I been in meetings all day."

"Any luck?"

"Luck? The world wasn't created by luck, Jimbo. By some lucky fuck waving his hands. There were plenty of meetings first. There were things to talk over, you bet. Hierarchies to set straight. Camera angles. Production budgets."

Miracle laughed, and Thompson saw a glint in the man's eyes, a tiny crack of light shimmering in the snowy depths.

"No, it was a long process. A lot of details. Adam and Eve, and that goddamn snake. That's what it took to create the world. Not a concept, but a plan. Divine inspiration." The light in Miracle's eyes opened wider and Thompson remembered the story about the gangster to whom Billy owed money, and how that gangster was not going to wait forever. He felt Miracle's nervousness and smelled his sweat. "Michele and I, we have someone coming down to talk to us. A money man."

"Here?"

"Yeah. So I can't talk as long as I might like." Miracle set Thompson's pages on the bar. "How much you need to finish this?"

Thompson stammered. He hadn't expected Miracle to jump into the money end so quick. "Eight," he said at last. "Half up front, half on close."

Miracle let out a whistle. "This is coming out of my pocket, you know."

"I can do it for six." Thompson's voice broke.

"Two. That's the best I can offer. I would do better if I could, but my financials are pretty fragile. Also, you need to guarantee me a publisher."

"How do I do that?"

"Tell 'em you got everything all lined up. Tell 'em its going to be blockbuster movie. I'll pay one-half up front, okay. Maybe the publisher will kick in more."

"If I'm going to do this right, I need to see your screenplay. I need to know the story."

Miracle waved him off. "Don't worry about all that. I've got everything you need, right here."

He took out a newspaper clipping and slid it to Thompson. It wasn't long, just a few inches of blotter copy about a man wanted in Texas for double murder. The fugitive had tied a man and woman back-to-back, cinching the knots so the ropes tightened as the couple struggled to get free. In the end, the couple had strangled in their chairs.

Thompson was puzzled. Then he realized: Miracle wanted him to use the newsclip as the basis for the story.

"There's your killer. He kills this couple in Texas, then he hightails it to Los Angeles."

"Why here?"

"He needs money, and there's this old man from his past, you see, an ex-con, a kind of father figure, who lives out this way. This old con, he sets our boy up with a murder contract in Hollywood."

Billy Miracle made a sweeping motion with his hands, slapping them together. "Kabam. That's it. How the stories come together. The killer. The love triangle. Behind the contract is a jealous woman. She wants her rival dead. And our boy from Texas—he's the instrument of her passion."

Miracle made it sound like a neat bit of business, but Thompson wasn't so sure.

"That's the truth about killers," said Miracle. "We act like they come out of the blue. Out of the deep dark nowhere. Fact is, we create them. All of us. That's what the *Manifesto's* about. That's what I want the audience to understand."

"All right," Thompson said. "One thing, though—money. I'm a little short."

"Find a publisher, and I'll have my people draw you a contract. Meantime, I've got to get back to Michele. Like I told you, we've got money on the line. Mr. Big, he's on his way."

Miracle went back to Michele Haze. She sat smoldering under the blue light. In the movies, she had played dozens of roles—a country girl, a city sophisticate, a tramp—but it was always the same part. A woman yearning for the good life, tormented by some inner darkness.

She and Jack Lombard had had a very public affair, off and on, never marrying, but it had gone on for years. Then recently things had begun to sour, not just with Lombard but on the screen too. Lines had begun to show on her face, and it took too much gel to hide them from the camera. Lombard had put her aside for The Young Lovely. So now she sat with Billy Miracle, lighting a cigarette, glancing toward her reflection in the darkening mirror.

Thompson finished his drink, grabbed up his bag with the cashmere sweater inside. He felt the liquor burning in his stomach, and a light-headedness upstairs.

The barroom door opened again. The light came tumbling in and a shadow emerged from that light. When the door closed, the shadow took the shape of a man. Jack Lombard.

Lombard was in his early fifties. He was a tall man, and stood with a boyish slouch. From a distance he struck you as nothing special. Just another someone, a guy with a casual manner, ordinary, but it was this ordinariness people found attractive. In his way, he was a good-looking man. Blondish hair, just turning gray, and eyes that were disarmingly blue.

Thompson remembered his own business with Lombard. He'd been hired to write the script of an adventure movie. Meanwhile Lombard maneuvered behind the scenes, the way producers do. A string of directors. Peckinpah and Hill and back to Peckinpah again. The project had ended on the cutting room floor in Mexico, with Peckinpah whipping out his dick, pissing on the roughcut. So Lombard had brought in another writer, and Thompson had lost his shot at the big money.

Now he watched Lombard shake Miracle's hand. He had a touch of hatred for the man, a touch of venom. He watched him kiss Michele Haze. Thompson didn't understand at first, then it occurred to him. Lombard was the money man Miracle had been waiting for. It didn't quite make sense. Lombard and Haze had split up, and he couldn't see Lombard dealing with the likes of Miracle. Yet Miracle had gotten past The Young Lovely and here they were, the three of them, Lombard and Haze and Miracle, all at the same table.

Thompson paid his bill and left. Outside, he stood blinking under the desert sun, clutching the red sweater inside its bag and wondering what to do next.

I should toss the sweater, he thought. It's the only link between myself and the dead girl. I could stuff it in the dumpster behind Musso's, or in the bushes around the corner. It was still daylight, though; he might be seen. Inside the bar, the girl's death had seemed remote, but now he wondered about her, and who she might have been. He felt again tainted with guilt. The sun was like a white light inside his head; he felt pain deep inside his stomach. He did not want to go back down to his room on the Strip, not now. A man emerged on the street ahead of him. He was tall and thin and moved with quick steps, angling through the street hustlers, coming at him through the rising fumes. The Okie, Thompson thought. The man wanted his keys back, his car, his corpse. But the man was not the Okie at all; he looked emptily at Thompson, crossed the street, kept on going.

Thompson felt the foreboding again, a trap about to spring. Planets misaligning, stars falling out of the sky.

He tried to shake the feeling. He staggered up the hill to the penthouse, where Alberta would be waiting, like she always waited, he told himself, scrubbed clean, in her dress with her string of pearls, and her hair done perfect, and while he thought about her, he caught again the fragrance of the sweater, and felt an erection growing against all odds, sadly, morosely, emerging from the nowhere like a tombstone from the grass.

SEVEN

HE FOUND ALBERTA IN THE LIVING ROOM. The light outside had begun to shift, and she looked pretty on the couch, in her loose cotton dress. He sensed the leanness of her body, and its softness too. Her face had aged, but unlike him, her muscles hadn't yet gone to hell. She didn't drink, and her eyes were still clear, though that clearness could be a sharpness sometimes, and her eyes seemed to strike everything she saw.

She smiled to herself, knowing he watched her. There was something alluring in that smile, something bitter.

"Honey?"

"Yes?"

"I've got good news." He sat down beside her and put his hand on her leg.

"What news is that?"

"We don't have to move."

"What do you mean?"

"I've got the deal all but made. With Miracle. It's a sure thing."

He'd drunk too much. It was a tricky business, to maintain your balance. To walk the old beam. Too little, you got the shakes. Too much, and the whole world shook. He'd waltzed along pretty well for quite a while since his last tumble, two years ago, maybe three, but now that beam was narrowing down.

"Your sister called from Lincoln."

Alberta got up angrily.

"What's the matter?"

"I broke a nail."

That wasn't it. She'd broken a million nails. She was

mad because they were leaving the penthouse. It all went back to that son of a bitch Lombard. If he hadn't scuttled me that first time around, I wouldn't be in this position now.

"Miracle's giving me two thousand."

"It's not enough. We still have to move."

"It will hold us over. Until something bigger."

"Something bigger's not coming."

"What do you expect me to do?"

"Why don't you have yourself a drink?"

"I haven't been drinking. I don't know how you could say something like that."

"No. You haven't been drinking. I don't have two feet. And birds don't fly. I see how it is."

For an instant, despite everything, he felt like murdering her. Pushing her off the cliff, into the gray Pacific.

"What did my sister want?"

He studied her face. Then he put his hand under her shift. In the old days, when they were younger, that would have been the end of it, they would have tumbled backwards onto the couch. Now the longer they sat there like that, his hands caressing her leg, the more still and quiet she became, until it seemed she was not breathing at all, and in that silence there was again that question she'd asked him the other day.

Why?

It wasn't just one question, but a million, and the answer seemed to rest in that space between her legs, where the light and dark were all mixed together.

She pushed his hand away.

"Your sister ran into that woman in Lincoln."

"What woman?"

"Lucille Jones. It seems she's on her way out here."

"To Los Angeles?"

"Convention business of some sort, she and her husband. They're staying at the Château, but Lucille, she's going to be there a few days, alone, before her husband comes out. At least that's the news from Franny."

He felt Alberta studying him, seeing how he would take this. If there might be something in his face to give him away. She had her suspicions.

"Lucille's husband, he's a big success," she said.

"What's he do?"

"A doctor of dentistry, you know that."

"Makes plenty of money, I bet."

"A fortune," she said.

"Gives half to charity, the other half to the church, and still has enough left over to live like a prince."

"You're just jealous."

"No, it's the other way around," said Thompson.

"What do I have to be jealous of?"

"Lussie married so well, and you, on the other hand . . ." He paused, feeling the knife in his heart, the pain a little more sharp, a little more sweet, because he had placed it there himself. He waited to see if she would pull the dagger out.

"Oh, I don't know about that," she said. "My husband—he's the best known writer in Los Angeles. Famous as the dirt. Desert Sands, that's his name. Mister Goddamn Desert Sands."

Thompson had had enough. He stomped out, taking the sweater with him, and also his flask of bourbon.

•

Outside, Thompson thought about the girl on Whitley Terrace, in the back of the Cadillac. He started to walk up the hill, feeling the same compulsion he'd felt earlier, but after a few steps he changed his mind. It would not be wise to go up there, and anyway gravity pulled a person down, not up. So he plummeted towards the Strip instead, to his little room and the typewriter on the table at the window. He didn't start to work, not right away. He wondered some more about the girl, and he drank. He drank until a white light filled his head. It was the black-out light, the light of nothingness. As it grew brighter, he remembered the sweater. He looked everywhere. On the closet floor, under the bed, in his dresser drawers. Maybe I stashed it on the hill, he thought. Or maybe. . . maybe something else. . . there is no sweater, no girl. I'm finally losing it, and she is just a figment of my imagination, another hieroglyphic in a line of hieroglyphics on the white and shimmering page.

EIGHT

It was a trap. The woman who picked me off the road, her name was Belle Lanier. She took me home and put me up in the spare bedroom, in her Daddy's house.

I took off my clothes and lay naked in the bed. I'd met her Daddy at dinner, and her little sister. The sister was a bit like Belle, only more wholesome, with big glasses, and a toothy smile. I touched myself, imagining both sisters at once. How, if I played things right, I could be their Daddy's right-hand man someday.

A plan was forming in my head.

Forget it boy, you ain't nothing but a small time con.

It was the voice again. Pops. The prison psychologist had told me not to mind him anymore. Said Pops was not real, no, only a voice in my head that I'd made up when I was a kid because I didn't have any dad of my own. Just all those men my mother used to bring around.

There was a knock on the door. Belle strolled in and sat on the bed. She wore a silk shift and a flower in her hair.

"My daddy's a rich man," she said.

Then she straddled my leg, so the warm ugly part of her was against my knees. She put her hand on me down low, pressing her lips over mine. I struggled against her a little bit, but she wouldn't let me go. I thought of her sister, the wholesome one, so it was like they were both with me at once. Belle kept her hand where it was until finally I let loose with everything inside and made a noise like an animal grunting around in the dark. Her lips curled then, like I had just proved something she knew all along. Then she left and I lay alone, listening to those crickets outside, and the cicadas and the whip-poor-wills and the katydids, all making a noise like the sound of the Texas night whipping through the windwing as you go roaring down the road, afraid to keep on going, afraid to stop.

NINE

THOMPSON WOKE UP IN THE AZTEC HOTEL. He felt better than he should feel—a little sore in the gut, a bit wobbly in the knees—but still well enough to find himself a copy of the morning paper. It was full of the usual grim business. Nothing about the girl in the Cadillac, though. If the police had found her corpse, the news of that discovery wasn't exactly shaking the town.

Everything will be all right, he told himself. Anyway, he had enough worries. Alberta for one. Money for another. He needed to finalize the deal with Billy Miracle; he needed a publisher.

He called his editor in New York, a young man by the name of Hector Sally.

"Who did you say you were?"

"Thompson. Jim."

The secretary grunted, impressed as hell. Then she put him on hold for a million years. A hundred million. The Ice Age came and went. Dinosaurs prowled once more the tar pits at La Brea. On Sunset Boulevard, under the tattered awnings, the figures of the waking world and Thompson's imagination intermingled. Here was the Okie. Here, Billy Miracle. Here, the Texas drifter, high stepping out of the pages of his novel.

Hector picked up. "Jim! How are you doing?"

"I have a deal. It's a book package tied to a movie. I thought you might want to know."

"Well, have your agent send me the manuscript."

"Forget my agent."

"We do have certain protocols, Jim."

Thompson tried to explain the deal he had going with Billy Miracle.

"I don't know," Hector said. "Your last book. Sales. . ."

"This has a tie-in already."

Hector hemmed around. He was an Ivy League kid who liked to think he was editing real literature. Only his bosses wanted sales, and to get sales it meant thrillers and good-looking heroes and a host of women just waiting to spread their legs. Morality at the end, though. A hero with a sense of dignity. Affirmation. Bad guys punished and the sluts all murdered.

"Let me talk to marketing. I'll call you back."

"You're not just saying that, are you, Hector?"

"I'm not that way."

"I didn't think you were that way."

"I'll call you."

"You promise?"

"I said I would, didn't I?"

"The heart of every good story's a good character," said Thompson.

"All right."

"I think this can be an important book."

"I'll talk to the folks upstairs."

"Important," he repeated, but Hector was gone.

•

Later, Thompson searched his hotel room again, looking for the sweater. What had happened last night, it had happened before. Time disappearing into light. A few minutes, maybe. Even a few hours. It was not just time that got lost. Objects, too. Usually, they would show up again. Where, though, when, he couldn't be sure.

He glanced up at the closet. On the high shelf, he had placed his father's gun, a stack of manuscript papers, clothes. Had he checked there?

Yes, last night, he was all but sure. He'd torn the place apart.

Franny was right, he told himself suddenly. She'd told him once: you made a mistake, all those years ago, marrying Alberta. He went now to the phone and dialed the Château. The operator put him through.

"Hello?"

It was her voice. A Midwestern accent. Eastern Nebraska, to be exact, the sound of a magpie disappearing into the bulrushes of the Platte River. It moved something in him, that innocuous voice of an older woman, past middle age. A voice you could can tomatoes with, you bet. It was Lussie, all right, but he couldn't respond. He was all tied up inside. All he could do was listen, his heart pounding. Then she rang off.

TEN

MUSSO'S WAS A REFUGE, A SECOND HOME. Not a perfect home, but good enough—cool and dark, away from the afternoon glare. That's where he was headed, again, walking along Hollywood Boulevard. The sun was bright and hot. It came at you with a white bounce, shimmering in the storefront windows. The light gleamed too in the passing windshields, and that gleam stayed in his eyes as he opened the door at last and pushed towards the bar. Musso's was dim and it took a while before his sight came back. He stood at the bar, sorting through shadows till his own face came clear—lips parted, white hair askew—in the mirror on the other side of the counter.

The bartender stood waiting.

"Whiskey," Thompson said. "And a beer back."

He had come to meet Billy Miracle, but he was not thinking about that now. He relinquished himself to memory. He bowed his head over the glass. The air conditioner was cool and for a minute he was back on the line, listening to Lussie's voice—the sound of apple cobbler, rosy cheeks, a dress fluttering up on a spring day—and in his reverie he was about to answer her, to say something into the phone.

He took a drink and let the moment pass.

Then he swiveled in his seat and noticed Michele Haze. She sat in a booth not far away, talking to a man. She wore white pumps and a white blouse. The man sat with his back to Thompson. He wore a cheap plaid shirt and slacks the color of coffee, and there seemed something familiar about him. In his gawkiness. In the way his feet splayed wide apart as he hunched insistently across the table.

Michele did not seem to be enjoying the man's company.

The man twisted in his seat, and Thompson caught him in profile. The buzz cut. The slack jaw. The hapless expression.

The Okie.

"I want my money," he said, and jabbed a finger at the movie star.

It was the voice of the heartland again, the motor puttering idiotically down the long rows of green, except now there was a whine to it, something caught in the gears.

The Okie jerked up from the table, head bobbing, his body rising to its feet so quickly Thompson didn't have time to react. Their eyes met in the mirror. Thompson hid his face in his drink. He felt his heart constrict, he worried he might stroke and die—but the Okie did not come. Apparently he had not recognized him. Then the man was gone, pushing out the door and into the street, strutting furiously into that desert light.

•

After the Okie had left, Thompson approached Michele Haze. She was a beautiful woman, but you could see the impending wreckage in the faint lines that weathered out from her eyes. They were dark eyes, almost black, with the memory of innocence in them, however slight and slumber-headed.

"Are you all right?"

"I'm fine, Mr. Thompson. My agent usually filters them out, the nuts and wackos, but they can be persistent. Sometimes they track you on their own."

Thompson did not know if he believed her explanation. She had recognized him, though, and he was pleased.

"You're here to meet Billy?"

"Yes," he hesitated. "I got the impression, the other day, Billy was pitching the movie to Lombard."

"Your impression was right."

He saw her vulnerability. She knew better than he the kind of stories going around: how Lombard had dumped her for the younger woman. She shrugged, as if reading his thoughts, dismissing them. When she spoke again, he noticed the faintest slur.

"Because of who we are, Jack and I, our life gets public. Everybody knows our transgressions."

Thompson didn't say anything. Though she looked right at him, when she spoke, he felt somehow as if he did not exist.

"And Jack, he's at the age where he wants light. Youth. But it's no different than the sort of thing that goes on with other couples. We've been through worse, and we've gotten back together."

She took a drag off her cigarette and gave him a look that he had seen in the pictures. It was the inward glance, reserved for interchanges with minor characters, at the moment when the star was revealing her inner thoughts. "The other night Billy and Jack and I were talking about the film. Billy may have got some ideas. But it wasn't from what Jack was saying. Billy was hearing what he wanted to hear."

"What do you mean?"

"The important thing isn't the picture. The important thing is Jack and I. Our relationship."

She gave Thompson a blunt look.

"We're getting back together."

Michele leaned back in the booth. Something in her manner suggested she did not quite believe her own words. She lifted her head, tracking something behind him. He heard footsteps, then felt a hand on his shoulder.

"Hey, Jimbo, how're you doing?"

It was Billy Miracle. He lowered himself into the booth next to Michele.

"We gotta deal. We're going to make a movie."

Miracle's tongue wandered across his lips. His skin was tanned, his hair sleek. He looked confident as hell, too confident. There's something out of whack, Thompson thought. Then Miracle sniffed, running a finger across his nostrils. Thompson was an old man, maybe, but he'd been around. He was wise. The rumors were true. Miracle had his nose in the powder.

Michele Haze, meanwhile, repositioned herself under the light, and he could no longer see the fine lines that feathered out from her eyes. Only blonde hair and high cheek bones and a face that looked as if it had been sculpted out of expensive stone.

"You have a deal?" Thompson asked.

"We got a handshake, don't we?" Miracle glanced in Michele's direction. "Isn't that right, baby?"

"There was a handshake, yes."

"Lombard?"

"That's right. Lombard."

Miracle slid some papers across the table.

"What's this?"

"Contract. We want you to do the book, Jack and I. We'd like that."

Thompson picked up the contract. He made a show of reading, but there was more action behind him.

Michele Haze stood up.

"Jack," she said softly, her voice full of aspiration.

It was old home week, it seemed, all the players circling into position. Lombard had returned. He seemed more delicate than he had the other night, though—thin and rakish, yes, but standing about with a skittishness that suggested he did not altogether want to be here.

Michele slid past Billy, out of the booth, and went to him. She stumbled and leaned into his chest. They kissed, but lightly. Lombard pulled away. She stuck with him, and they went together towards the bar. Billy Miracle, meanwhile, watched with concern. Lombard had not so much as nodded in his direction.

"Of course, there are still some details to work out," he said.

"What about Lombard's girl friend?" asked Thompson. "I thought she wouldn't let you through."

"She and Jack, they had some kind of quarrel. The Young Lovely, she was getting ready to go out of town, a trip home. Then she found out about our meeting. About Michele and I—and the picture. She went through the roof. Left town in a tizzy, a couple days back. No one's seen her since."

A suspicion rose in Thompson's mind, the sensation there was something beneath the surface, something he should grasp. He'd had the sensation before, events unfolding, moving towards one another, then away—like head lamps careening through a dark intersection on Wilshire, almost colliding, then vanishing into the city.

"Where did you say she went, The Young Lovely?"

"Home. A cornfield, I believe. In Iowa. Or maybe it was Ohio. No matter, she was wearing a gingham dress."

"She'll be back?'

The producer pushed the contract toward him once again. There was a check attached. A thousand dollars. Thompson faltered. He knew he should send the contract to his agent first. In the meantime, though, the deal might disintegrate. He could lose the money in front of him now. Be patient, he told himself. Wait.

He signed.

"We should celebrate," said Miracle. "Take a toast."

"In a minute."

"Where are you going?"

"I have to get some air. I'll be right back." In truth, Thompson wanted to get to the bank. He had made a mistake, maybe, signing the contract, but he still meant to get the check cashed.

"Don't be gone long. Jack's coming over to the table any minute. We'll drink to our success."

The opposite appeared to be true. Michele and Lombard were separating at the bar.

Miracle rose to his feet.

"Jack," he called. "Jack!"

Miracle caught the other man at the rear door, on the other side of the restaurant. The two men stood close, but it was easy to see Lombard's discomfort. Miracle put a hand on his shoulder. Lombard shrugged it off. He said something then, Lombard did. Thompson was too far to hear the words, but the expression on the man's face was one of disgust. His glance took in not just Billy but Michele too, all in white, eyes downcast. She tugged at her blouse.

Lombard pushed his way through the door.

Miracle rocked back on his heels, stunned, then he too gave Michele a dirty glance—and bulled out into the rear lot, looking to save his deal.

ELEVEN

THOMPSON MADE HIS EXIT THROUGH THE FRONT DOOR. Miracle's check had been drafted on an account at Security Bank, across from Graumann's Chinese. The way things were unraveling, he did not trust the deal to hold.

"You wish to deposit this in your account, sir?"

"No. I want cash."

"Identification?"

Thompson laid out his driver's license and his Guild Card on the counter.

"Could you put the money in an envelope, please?"

The teller did as he was asked. Thompson didn't want to go back to Musso's, nor to the Aztec Hotel. He thought of Lussie, over at the Château, but he was not ready for her either. He lingered on Highland Avenue, in the shadow of the Revlon building, where inside a beautician tinkered with an old woman's hair.

At the intersection, two cars all but collided. The drivers cursed and yelled. A prostitute strutted by. Two friends slapped hands on the corner, hipsters in dirty jeans. The drivers went on cursing. Mid-block, across the way, the prostitute found her mark: a nobody with a light in his eyes.

It was rush hour and things were happening. Accidents. Chance meetings. Heavenly bodies colliding.

What had the Okie been doing with Michele Haze?

There had been another address on the back side of that paper, he remembered.

Thompson went up Orange Street, which had been true to its name once upon a time, all those sweet trees blossoming between farmhouses out here in the desert nothing. Now the road was lined with parking lots and the back entrances to hotels that sagged and crumpled and smelled vaguely of starlets who'd been screwed on the casting couch a couple million times but never got the job.

Thompson felt sorry for the dead woman.

He crossed Franklin, skittering up the street to the Hillcrest Arms. Inside, he found the paper still on the mantle.

The El Rancho, 87 Palm Avenue, #4.

On the other side of the paper was the address of the Hillcrest apartment, written in the same hand. Thompson hesitated. It's not my job to investigate things. I'm an old man. Then he thought of the dead girl, her body curled in the back of the trunk. Once again it were as if he were hovering over her, studying her bruised corpse, clutching the key in his hand.

Old busybody, old fool.

He called himself a cab.

•

The El Rancho was a wartime motel, built on the cheap, that sat in a neighborhood of two-door bungalows, on the edge of Echo Park. Overhead a flickering sign gave off a light resembling the sun at dusk.

Thompson paid the driver to wait, and got out of the cab.

The Okie had come for a pay-off, Thompson figured. He'd killed the girl, and he'd come to Hillcrest to deliver the corpse, to show he'd done the job he was supposed to do. There'd been a screw-up, though. The Okie was no professional, and he'd taken the corpse to the wrong address.

The Okie was supposed to have come here, to the El Rancho.

But what was my address doing on the other side of the paper? Thompson wondered. And who was Sydney Wicks?

Meanwhile, the desk lady saw him coming. She was about fifty, dyed blonde. Maybe she had been a charmer once, but she'd spent too much time standing behind that desk, watching clients check in, check out. All that in-and-out had given her a sour look.

"You want a room?"

"No. I was supposed to meet someone. A man named Sydney Wicks."

"Not tonight. We've got no one by that name."

"Could you check last Monday?"

"Why for? Monday's come and gone."

"I lost my appointment book, and I can't remember whether I was supposed to meet him last Monday, or today. He's a client and I'm afraid maybe I missed him. Could you check?"

The woman smirked. The look on her face said she knew he was lying, but she flipped back through the registry anyway, running her ugly fingers down the page.

"Yeah. Checked in Tuesday afternoon."

"Do you remember what he looked like?"

"I should remember? He's your client."

"We only met once."

"You a cop?"

"Do I look like a cop?"

She eyed him up and down. "No. You don't look like anything." Her glance was obscene. She drummed those fingers on the counter, ran them through her hair. Smiled.

"Did you see him?"

"No. I wasn't working the desk that day."

"Who was?"

"Julie."

"How can I find her?"

"She's history. Made the big connection."

"What does that mean?"

"Honeymoon. A sudden thing. You know how it is with the young. They fall so quickly in love."

"When will she be back?"

"She quit. No forwarding address."

"That's too bad."

"A regular shame. A fool for love, that girl. To leave a job like this."

She gave him the look again, like she'd seen one too many of his kind—and wanted to take it out on the next man available, spending the next ten years with him in a cramped apartment, serving him dinner in her night-gown.

"Well—thanks, anyway," he said

"Sure, buster. My pleasure."

•

Outside, the traffic was thick. In the back of the taxi, he took some money from the bank envelope and transferred it into his wallet. Then he noticed something else. His identification was missing.

He'd left it at the bank, at the teller's cage when he cashed Miracle's check.

It had been a bad couple days

Finally, the traffic let loose. He had the taxi let him off on Hollywood and Argyle, not far from the Aztec. There was action on the avenue. Long legs and leather pants. Dayglo skirts and the sound of engines, a line of lights idling slowspeed under the palms. The sky was red. He went into the bar on the corner and had a whiskey, up raw, no ice. In that first sip he tasted the glow of the evening, the blackness descending. He loved that taste, he told himself, and he drank until it was gone from the glass.

TWELVE

AN HOUR LATER, THOMPSON WALKED out under the hanging neon into the street. Darkness had descended, but the city was lit up, hazy as could be. The sky overhead was gray-black, smudged with yellow. Some drunks nearby hollered like animals. Thompson kept moving. A woman sat on the corner, coughing blood. Outside the Aztec Hotel, a pink town car was parked at the curb, facing the wrong direction, into traffic.

The driver's door swung open.

"Get in, Jim"

He tried to object, but it was too late. Miracle twisted his arm.

"We've got some celebrating to do, remember?"

"I need to get to work. The book."

"Don't be a spoilsport."

Miracle nudged him into the back, and Thompson saw Michele in the passenger's seat, slumped low. No reason to be afraid, he told himself.

"Did you talk to Jack?"

"Sure," said Miracle. "I talked to him."

Miracle reached into the glove compartment, pulled out a bottle, a glass. He fumbled about with them for quite awhile, clumsying around on the seat.

"Lean back, Jim. Relax. I'll fix you a drink."

Thompson did as he was told, and eventually Miracle passed him a drink.

"We're going to paint the town, us three."

"You can me drop me off," Michele said. "I've got to be up early."

"Don't be silly."

Miracle careened into traffic, and Thompson sipped the whiskey. It had a metallic afterbite—the cheap stuff.

"What happened with Jack?" Thompson asked.

No onc answered, and Thompson suspected things had gone badly. The movie deal had exploded.

"What happened after I left?" he asked again.

"Jack left," Michele said. Miracle shot her a look that said be quiet, don't say a goddamn word—but she went on. "Then Billy went after him."

"And?"

"Then Billy came back."

"Don't worry about the details, Jimbo," Miracle interrupted. "Things are coming together. Lombard's high on this project. We're all high."

Thompson caught a glimpse of Michele in the rear view mirror. Her face was a mess. She dabbed at her compact. Her eyes had the same dark sheen as always, maybe darker, shimmering absently in the passing light. Her head wobbled. She had been drinking, but it was not just that. Those eyes, they were not the eyes of a drunk.

He thought about the faint slur that was always there, even in the movies. The way she clutched her purse.

Valium, he thought. The old heart stopper. A starlet's best friend.

"Remember that book of yours," said Miracle, "where the hero kills his sweetheart? Then blames it on some fool passing by. Remember that?"

Thompson finished the whiskey. He felt black-headed. Miracle was jumbling things up, as usual, but still, things like that happened in his books. A dumb slob screwed by happenstance, over and over. Maybe the slob wasn't altogether innocent, but the punishment, well, it made you wonder.

Miracle went on. "The fool takes it in the shorts, if I remember right. Gets blamed for the whole business."

"Where are we going?"

"Tell me, Jim, there's always a place in your stories, things just go haywire. I can't tell what the hell's happening."

It was true. Events got skewed. Characters stumbled into the abyss.

"What's your point?"asked Thompson.

"Jack Lombard and I, we had things in common. Men of vision. Different visions, maybe—but still, you get the drift. Successful men are like gangsters. In control. Powerful. Ruthless. You, Jimbo, on the other hand, you."

The blackness was overcoming him. It wasn't his usual blackness, but something more powerful. They were way out Sunset now. Miracle still driving, but his voice close by, somehow, hissing in his ear. "Lombard expressed some concerns, Jim. Said you have no control. Just down and down you go. Then out. You never make it back."

Thompson tried to shake Miracle's voice from his head.

They stopped at a light. Near Sunset Plaza—a corner joint, tables on the sidewalk. The kind of place tourists went to watch movie stars, and ended up watching the traffic instead. He grabbed at the door handle.

"Hey, where you going? Jim?"

Thompson lurched onto the street. He heard Miracle coming after him. Horns blared.

"Come on, Jim. Let's get back into the car."

"Fuck you," Thompson said. "Fuck Lombard!" He bellowed, thrashing among the tables. He slipped, and he threw his arm out to catch his balance. A table tipped. A chair fell over. Thompson leaned against a lamppost and slid.

"What's the matter with him?" someone asked, a bystander.

The noise from the horns was wild now. Footsteps, voices rising among the horns. People gathering to see the problem. Miracle shooing them off.

"No, no. Not to worry. Just too much to drink, huh Jimbo. We'll give this boy a ride home. Come on, Michele. Give me a hand."

Billy Miracle crouched on one side of him, Michele Haze on the other. They cooed and cajoled and promised to take him home and Thompson did not have the legs to resist. He stood in the center, an arm draped over each of them. They helped him along and for a moment it wasn't so bad. Thompson leaned his head towards the movie star, catching the heavy smell of her perfume, burying his head in her platinum hair. She grunted under his weight, surprisingly strong, then his feet buckled, wobbling, and for a minute it seemed he would pitch forward onto the asphalt. Somehow they maneuvered him back to the car.

"Take me home."

"Sure, Jim, sure."

They gave him a push, and Thompson slumped into the back seat. The horns fell quiet. He surrendered to that blackness, and for a minute he was way down in it, then he struggled back up, pressing his head to the window. They were rounding a corner, up into Beverly Hills. He wanted to protest, but he couldn't. It was like there was something stuffed inside his mouth. He heard a voice, small as hell, way down there, somewhere in the dark. Thompson tried answering and heard himself mumbling, and it was the same voice he mumbled as he read over and over the typewritten words on the page, when he was on the cusp of two worlds. Now he was back up above the blackness and he heard Miracle and Haze arguing. Thompson could not make out the words. He listened for them, but it was a like viper language, way down in there, and he was pursing it, plummeting towards that darkness, and then they were helping him walk again, one on either side. He buried his face in Michele's blouse. He looked up and saw in her face the intense beauty of someone carried along by an evil she could not control. Their eyes met. He reached for her. In that instant she let him loose, her and Miracle both, letting him fall hard into the darkness, through it, disappearing, plummeting toward the black earth.

THIRTEEN

THOMPSON WOKE AT DAWN. The sky overhead was a wild pink—and nearby, in a cypress hedge, some starlings were making a fuss, flitting blackly from branch to branch.

The remains of some vast darkness lingered in his head. The darkness was a lake, but it was a lake that had no shore, and there were no sounds and no reflections rippling across its surface. He did not want to return to that lake, but return he did.

He opened his eyes again later. How much later, he could not say. The starlings were gone and the sun more fierce. Though it was still morning, and the ground still cold, the desert sun burned overhead.

He lay in front of a very large house: a mansion in the contemporary style, all windows and aluminum and enameled steel. He worried someone might come to those windows, but no one did. The air was still and quiet and hot. His head hurt. He wondered if he had died and this were some uncharted circle of hell, reserved especially for himself.

A car rolled into the drive. He lay as still as he could, flattening himself into the grass. The car was a late-model sedan, nothing fancy. Out stepped a Mexican woman in a white uniform. She did not glance in his direction but sauntered primly down the pink flagstones to the rear of the house.

The maid, Thompson figured. And he realized he had not died after all. He was in Beverly Hills.

•

Thompson scrambled towards a gap in the hedge, hobbling. The branches scratched his face, but he pushed through. On the other side, he hobbled some more; he had lost a shoe. He searched the hedge a while, then started down the hill. Maybe his shoe lay back on the grass, but he did not want to be caught loping about on some movie star's lawn.

What happened last night? he wondered.

He had experienced blackouts before, but usually after a long night of drinking. Last night, he had barely begun.

He patted himself down, found the bank envelope in his jacket pocket, money intact—but his wallet gone. It had been empty anyway, no identification, so in that matter, at least, he had lucked out.

The hill bottomed at Sunset, and he crossed to the bus stop. After a little while a cop car drove by, then another, each turning up the way Thompson had just come, back up Beverly Drive. The cops had their sirens off, but they drove with a degree of urgency.

The cops could be investigating anything, he told himself. A tourist in Bob Hope's swimming pool. Doris Day's orgasms. Zsa Zsa's missing poodle.

Finally, the bus arrived. It was a local and took him a little ways past Sunset Plaza. Lately this part of the Strip had been taken over by the hippies. Suburban riff-raff, ghetto trash, aspiring actors, they wandered together up and down the street, all roaming about. At first glance it seemed they were mingling, engaged in some common enterprise. Up close, he realized they were each going their separate ways: hustling dope; buying bikinis, black lights, banana-colored slacks. Sitting at the open-air tables, eyes dim and glassy. Tapping the table tops with their fingertips and looking about, waiting for what was happening to happen. Washed up flotsam. Debris. Scum floating on a sea of nothingness. More all the time. They lounged in front of the Whiskey-A-Go-Go all night in their leather, then huddled under the billboards by day, passing their joints back and forth while overhead, painted and peeling, a giant blonde lounged beside a bottle of gin. Meanwhile the cars rolled by spewing exhaust, and Thompson felt himself, watery, dissolute, with an erection growing up suddenly, ridiculously, out of all this nothingness. An old man's erection, nothing to write home about—unless, of course, you were an old man yourself. Down Sunset, the Hollywood bus was nowhere to be seen.

He stepped into a notions shop and bought himself some sneakers and a clean shirt. The shirt was wide-collared, bright and gaudy, but it least it was not soaked through with sweat.

He started to walk, just to be moving. He would catch the bus at the next stop along the line. Further on, he glanced up and saw the Château.

Lussie was staying here.

In the old days the Château had been a glamorous joint, and the tour agents used that glamour now to attract out-of-towners and conventioneers. Thompson decided what the hell. He would cross the street and walk into the lobby. He would ring her room. If what Alberta had told him was true, her husband would not be in town for a few days yet.

The last time he'd seen Lussie had been in a hotel room in New York, maybe fifteen years back. He'd been in town trying to set up a book deal, and she had been on a business trip with her husband. The old man had been out for the day, so Thompson had gone up and knocked on her door.

She had opened up and let him in. Her eyes had flashed with something that surprised him. He wondered if it would be there again.

No, he told himself.

He couldn't go to the Château. Not in this state, disheveled as he was.

Thompson caught the bus back to the Aztec Hotel. He walked though the lobby, past the snoozing clerk, upstairs to his room.

He wanted out. Away from Billy Miracle. All these years writing about murderers and their victims, men trapped by their desires—by swell-looking babes and no account virgins—and now here he was, trapped too. He wasn't so different from the drifter in the book he was writing maybe, working his way toward a fatc scrawled in someone else's hand. But he went ahead anyway and sat down at his desk. He was under contract, after all.

FOURTEEN

Belle Lanier could get her old man to dance naked in the street, if that's what she wanted, so getting me the job at her father's place was a pretty straightforward business.

Daddy Lanier treated me like a prince. He paid me fair, and patted me on the back, and didn't seem to want anything in return. Maybe he was a good man like he seemed. Or maybe he was a fool.

Either way, my plan, it was to take these people for a ride. To milk them good and be on my way.

Then one day the younger sister, Gloria, showed up at the office. She wore her hair tied back and a brand new dress: a wide-collared thing that hung down below the knees. She had sincerity written all over her face.

"Hi," I said, and gave her my brightest grin. "What can I do for you?"

I took her for a stroll, and talked it up big. I told her how much I loved the town, and the people here, how it reminded me of my childhood. It was all lies, but she smiled, sweet as sap, and for a little while I believed my own words.

Finally we went back to the office. I looked through the window, watching her walk. I thought for a minute how I wished everything was good and wholesome as she made it seem. Just then I felt a hand on my shoulder. It was Daddy Lanier. He had been watching me study his youngest daughter as she strolled away under the pecan trees.

"You want to come over to dinner?"

He looked at me with the eyes of the father I'd never had. The good father. Who cared for me and wanted to see me do well in the world. Who would never treat me like that lousy voice in my head.

FIFTEEN

THE NEXT DAY, THOMPSON got a call from Matthew Roach, his agent in New York. They'd known each other for twenty years, back to the days when Thompson wrote for the crime magazines. Thompson liked hearing from him: the cheering lilt in his voice, all camaraderie, like a pat on the back that said:

Give 'em hell, buddy. They're all bastards, but hey, you, Mr. Million Bucks, you got what it takes.

The truth was, Roach was a swindler like all the rest. They'd fallen out a dozen times over the years, but none of that mattered. Thompson liked him anyway.

"Too bad about Jack Lombard. A damn shame." Roach's voice sounded odd. He wants something, Thompson thought. But why is he bringing up Lombard?

"Nothing's too bad for him. That son of a bitch."

"That's a hell of a thing to say."

"I'm a hell of a guy."

"The reason I called, Hector Sally talked to me, about your book deal. I think we can make this thing swing."

Thompson hesitated. He had hoped to do this without Roach, to save himself the commission. "Hector says they'll do the book. Contingent on the film. Any advance you get, though, that has to come from the production house."

"I was hoping. . ."

"That's the best I can get you."

Roach's voice was firm, and Thompson felt his old dislike of the man returning. He enjoyed the feeling. It felt good to hate his agent again. To hate agent and publisher at the same time, in the same moment, this was one of life's true pleasures.

"Now, this is what I want you to do. Send me a copy of the deal you have with Miracle."

"All right."

"You haven't signed it yet, have you?"

"No," Thompson lied.

"Good. Because I want to protect the rights on this. Send me the deal memo now, and the chapters as you write them. I'll forward the chapters to Hector. Meantime, I'll call my movie contacts. That way, if things fall through with Miracle, you'll still have the book, and maybe we can build something on that."

"All right."

Despite everything, Thompson enjoyed having Roach on the line. While he had him, he felt connected. He could smell Manhattan: the gray buildings and the grime, the perfumed blouses in elevators that never stopped rising, the presses inked up and ready to roll.

"So the place must be buzzing with it?" Roach sounded again as he had sounded when he first called, his voice heavy with insinuation.

"Buzzing with what?"

"What happened to Jack. Everybody must be talking. A dirty business like that."

"What dirty business?"

"You don't know?"

"No."

"Lombard was murdered."

Thompson felt his heart in his throat. "Murdered?"

"In Beverly Hills. In that big ass house of his. Someone beat him to death with a baseball bat."

"I didn't know."

"They found him upstairs. Whoever it was, they made a mess of it. Chased him all over the house."

"Jesus."

"It wasn't what you would call a clean kill. The man really suffered."

Thompson felt that big blackness inside him again, and he tried to remember what had happened the night before. He saw himself climbing out of Miracle's car, stumbling about those tables, and then he was inside the car again, heading into the hills.

After awhile, Roach got off the phone. Thompson sat himself in front of the typewriter, but it was hopeless. He went down to the newsstand and bought himself a copy of the *Herald.*

HOLLYWOOD MOGUL MURDERED
Bloody Crime Shocks Tinseltown

The body of movie mogul Jack Lombard was found early this morning beaten and bloodied almost beyond recognition in the foyer of his Beverly Hills mansion.

The body was discovered by Lombard's maid, Julia Alveraz, about 11:30 yesterday morning, according to Los Angeles police.

Mrs. Alvarez told police that the back door of Lombard's downstairs office was ajar, and there were signs a violent struggle had taken place.

Lombard was known to meet with producers, writers and directors at all hours of the night in his famed downstairs room, where some of the most celebrated movies in Hollywood history were conceived.

Though details at this time are sketchy, police said it appears the struggle began downstairs. Papers and household fixtures had been knocked on the floor, and a chair overturned.

After the initial attack, Lombard then fled his attacker, going upstairs into the mansion's large and spacious living room, which itself resembles a Hollywood stage set, filled as it is with props, costumes, antique cameras, and other memorabilia.

Here, Lombard apparently put up a fierce struggle for his life. Investigators say the room was in shambles, with much of the memorabilia broken and smashed.

Lombard's body was found just a few steps from the front door.

There were bloody hand prints on the vestibule walls, suggesting he had been on the verge of escape when the assailant cornered him at the entrance.

His head had been struck repeatedly with a blunt item. A bloody baseball bat was found nearby.

As there was no evidence of forced entry, investigators suspect the attacker may have been someone known to Lombard.

Lombard was a controversial figure who made and broke many careers in Hollywood. He was someone about whom people often felt passionately.

"At this point, we're following every lead we get," said Detective Orville Mann of the Los Angeles Police. "No one in Hollywood is beyond suspicion."

On an inside page, the newspaper had run a picture of Lombard's mansion. Thompson recognized the place immediately. He felt the dread rise inside him. All that glass, those steel rafters. He'd woken up there this morning, on the lawn, under those huge and sightless windows.

SIXTEEN

NOW THOMPSON STUDIED HIMSELF in the reflection of the newsstand window: his wrinkled trousers and his ridiculous shirt and the oversized sneakers. His face was lined like the face of an old bluff that had been soaked by rain and carved up by some bitter wind. He tried to light a cigarette, but his hands shook. He couldn't get control. He stepped off the street, into a bar. It was a skid row place. Inside, old men like himself were already into it, heads bowed, nodding toward their glasses. Sometimes they mumbled, whether to one another or to the drinks they held in their hands, it was hard to tell. The sounds those lips made were incoherent, but such incoherence was the point. Failed marriages. Childhood beatings. Loved ones killed by accident or in homicidal rage. These things happened. If you were deemed guilty, you might get locked up for a while. You might get lobotomized, or incarcerated alongside a man who longed for nothing more than to fuck your ass three times a week, but sooner or later society forgot about you. There were other matters, other criminals to punish. Anyway, maybe you did the job better yourself. So they let you go, and you wandered free and you needed the potion of forgetfulness.

"A whiskey," Thompson said.

The whiskey helped calm him. I'm innocent, he thought. And for a minute, the whiskey still hot in his belly, he believed it was true. He hadn't been a lousy husband, a lousy father. (So lousy, in fact, that his two daughters, his son, hell, their faces vanished on him, and all that was left were their eyes, boring up out of the nothing, out of the dark, lingering around like a question someone had forgotten to answer.)

He thought of his sister's place in La Jolla. She and her husband were in Lincoln, the house empty. He saw himself there by the ocean, recuperating in the salt air, finishing his book. He would go, he decided. Rest. And think things through.

As he stood up, he glanced into the mirror over the bar. It was not unlike the mirror at Musso's, except the glass here had gone bad. The reflection was no good, the image smoky and dark. He could not see himself clearly, and it was as if he had slipped over some boundary. He remembered Billy Miracle—his eyes in the rearview, his hands below the seat fiddling, then coming up with the drink. Miracle had been inside Michele's purse, Thompson realized. Then it occurred to him:

I was doped.

Thompson thought about the ride away from Sunset Plaza. Haze and Miracle dragging him into the darkness. Letting him fall.

They hired the Okie to kill the girl. They killed Lombard. And now they're trying to blame the whole business on me.

It was either that, or believe he'd gone over the edge himself.

SEVENTEEN

ON THE CORNER, NEAR THE OLD ROOSEVELT HOTEL, a clean-up crew was going at it, young men on their hands and knees, polishing those Hollywood stars embedded in the walkway. It was late morning, and the T-shirt shops and the pizza stands were just opening. A bouncer from one of the sex palaces hosed the walk nearby. The pigeons cooed, and the air was redolent with the smell of burned tomatoes and beer gone flat

Thompson thought about the girl in the Cadillac, and how her ringlets fell so sweetly over the bruised cheeks. He headed up Grace Avenue toward the Ardmore. His plan was to grab the keys to the Ford, then be on his way, to the coast.

He reached Franklin. All he had to do was go around the corner, and he would be home. He glanced up the hill toward Whitley Terrace, wondering if the Cadillac was still there, the girl curled in the trunk.

A patrol car pulled over the rise. A couple of young blues sat in the front seat. The cops were everywhere, it seemed, watching your every move. The one in the driver's seat gave him a little wave of the hand, telling him to cross. He went ahead, obliging the cop—going in a direction he had not intended to go. Up the hill, towards the Cadillac. Meanwhile, he felt the cops looking him over. He could guess what kind of sight he made. An old man in sagging pants and a knit shirt. I worked the Texas oil fields, Thompson wanted to tell them. I hung out with the Wobblies, I hopped the rails. It was what men did during the depression. Not just me, but thousands, all looking for work to feed the wife and kids back home. A person my own age, why, he would recognize that. These young cops, these nobodies, why. . .

The road climbed steeply. Thompson heard the squad car down below him, idling in the intersection. He worried somebody had seen him coming off Beverly Drive, and reported his description. The cops could be listening to it right now. Two seconds, the big red lights would come on. And here he'd be, cornered by happenstance.

At the top of the hill, he braved a look back.

The squad car was gone.

He stood on Whitely Terrace, alone, on a rise looking down toward the Ardmore and the rest of Hollywood. Just around the corner, the asphalt turned to gravel.

Maybe the Cadillac was still there. Either way it would be foolish to go see. The cops could be on a stake out, for all he knew.

He would not be standing here if that young cop had not motioned him to cross the street. Coincidence, inevitability—he wondered if there were a difference—compelled him forward. He stopped. His hands trembled. Maybe the Cadillac had never had been there at all. The incident was a dream, a drunken hallucination. Then why not go forward, under the eucalyptus. Down the gravel road. Dismiss it once and for all. But he wasn't that far off the beam, not yet. He'd seen the girl. Thinking about her, he all but saw her again. He could see too the empty trench further down the hill, and the shovel in the trunk.

The air tremored with unfinished business.

No!

A shiver ran through his body. The world shimmered and the leaves whispered. Then he pulled himself together and hurried down the hill. He would gather his things and go to the coast. Escape.

•

Inside the Ardmore penthouse, Thompson rummaged for some clean clothes, and for the key to the Ford. The apartment itself had the look of a world about to be forsaken. There were boxes stacked all about, and Alberta's clothes lay strewn on the bed. He went to his closet and took among other things the white jacket he'd worn years ago to the premier of *The Killing,* a movie he'd written with Stanley Kubrick. The son of a bitch.

Alberta wasn't anywhere around. Out on an errand, he guessed. Himself, he was going to the ocean.

He lugged his suitcase to the elevator. Outside, he found the Ford parked at the rear of the building, gleaming under the thin shade of a giant yucca, but its engine wouldn't turn for him. It made an unhappy noise that grew steadily fainter and died away.

Then he saw Alberta emerge from Mrs. Myers' green sedan. Mrs. Myers emerged too, a neighbor woman with whom Alberta sometimes went shopping—and the pair stood talking. Alberta wore a white blouse and black slacks. She held her hands up on her hips, and her breasts jutted against her white blouse. It was a posture he'd seen hundreds of times, and it always stirred his desire.

The women sauntered on towards the door. At the last minute, Alberta turned on her heels, as if surveying the parking lot.

Thompson was tempted to call out. In the old days, they would fight and afterwards it would be okay. They'd cuddle like teenagers, full of syrup, full of endearments:

Honey pumpkin. Sweet Dick. Lover girl. Joy of my life. Girlie puss.

Now she disappeared into the building. She did not

see him, and he did not call out. Maybe, because in the back of his head somewhere he was thinking of Lussie Jones, imagining her in the seat beside him as he made his way down the shore.

He tried the car. The engine wouldn't turn. The motor was silent as the dead.

He struggled the suitcase down the hill, sweating fiercely. Getting out was not so easy. On Hollywood Boulevard, he stepped again over all those stars embedded in the crumbling sidewalk. The clean-up crew was finished. The streets were empty and hot.

EIGHTEEN

BACK AT THE HOTEL, the desk clerk was stoned. His head lolled, and his eyes were shiny. He wore a jacket of the type worn by organ monkeys, only more frayed. The red fabric was matted by age, its color bleached by the sun, and the gold braid was all but worn from the sleeves. The jacket, too, had its own odor about it. It gave the young man the combined smell of the many men who had worn it before, then left it to hang, unwashed, in the bell clerk's closet.

"Messages?" Thompson asked.

"Huh?"

"Letters. Notes. Stationery scrawled with lipstick. Has anybody been by to see me?"

"Yeah. But nobody with lipstick."

"Who?"

"A man."

"Did he leave his name?"

"No."

"Did you ask for it?"

"Hey, I buzzed your room. When you didn't pick up, I told him to go knock on your door."

"Tell me, kid. What the hell's in your head?"

"Nothing. He gave me a tip."

"What happened to him?"

"What do you mean?"

"The man who was here, where did he go?"

"He waited around in the lobby for a while."

"Then?"

"He said he'd be back later."

"What did he look like?"

"I don't remember."

"What do you mean, you don't remember?"

"He gave me a tip, that doesn't mean I memorized his face." The kid squinted, as if looking up at Thompson from inside a dark hole. "Maybe you should loosen up."

Thompson had had it. "Go drown, you little rat." He wanted to smack the kid, but instead he burst into a coughing fit. The fit racked his body with a spasm that started deep in his lungs and seemed for an instant as if it would never stop.

The kid smirked. Thompson wanted to punish him. Instead, he went upstairs. He wondered who had come to see him. If the Okie had searched him out somehow, there was nothing to stop him from coming back in the middle of the night. The door lock was a flimsy piece of business.

He thought of his sister's place, and Lussie Jones. He called Greyhound, but the next bus wasn't till tomorrow morning. He thought about Lussie again. The way things were going, he might not have another chance to see her. He went to his closet and got out some studio stationery. He still had courier privileges from his time working with Colossal. One thing about the studios: If they were slow about giving you something, they could be just as slow about taking it away.

Dear Lussie,

My sister gave me your message. Yes, I would be most glad to see you again, perhaps show you around the City of Angels. I will be at the Musso & Frank Grill tonight, sixish, for drinks and dinner. It's a grand old place, dingy in the manner of the true Hollywood. If you are not otherwise engaged, I would love to have you at my table.

Yours,

J. Thompson.

Six o'clock was less than three hours away. It was not much notice, but maybe she would come. Meanwhile, the heat was stifling; he went to the window to get what he could of the breeze. Outside, the scofflaws had taken to the doorways and alleys, camping in the shadows. The Okie was still out there on the streets, Thompson figured. Sooner or later he would run into him again. There were laws about such things. Rules of nature. An object in motion tended to stay in motion. All lines intersected, all paths converged. Somewhere, past the curve of the ocean, Sepulvada ran into Sunset ran into Santa Monica Boulevard, became one street, divided again, became many.

A knock sounded on the door.

"Who's there?"

"Lieutenant Mann, Los Angeles Police."

Thompson glanced out the landing toward the fire escape. If he were a young man, he might leap out and be gone, but he was not a young man. He opened the door.

•

Lieutenant Mann was a plainclothes cop, tall and gangly. He wore a seersucker jacket, pressed slacks and a pink shirt that opened at the collar. He wore a white hat too, which he removed from his head as he stepped inside. The room was a mess. It smelled of whiskey and cigarettes and rumpled bed clothes, and Thompson's traveling case stood out in plain view. The cop took it all in without a flicker.

"You're originally from Oklahoma, I understand," said Lieutenant Mann. He made it sound like small talk, but Thompson knew better. If the cop knew this much, he knew more. He'd been checking into his background.

"Years ago."

"I spent some time on the force in Oklahoma City, but I'm from corn country myself."

"That right?"

"Cedar Rapids."

Once again Thompson heard it, the reedy accent of the Midwest. It shouldn't have surprised him. They were coming out here everyday, these Midwesterners, bringing with them their big ears, and their fat heads, and all that empty space in-between. Thompson had been through Cedar Rapids. He remembered the red brick hotels and the sandstone apartments and the huge silos, and he remembered too the oats mounded up on boxcars that rattled through town in a line that reached all the way to Dubuque. The cop's voice sounded a little like that, all those boxcars loaded with oats, rolling through the night.

"I hear you're a writer. A crime novelist, that right?" Mann flashed him an aw shucks smile. "Mind if I sit down?"

"Go right ahead."

The lieutenant made himself comfortable. Thompson waited for the grilling to begin, but Lieutenant Mann took his time. He was in no hurry to go anywhere, as if he were on a front porch back home, watching the cars roll by on Main Street, waving to the men in their overalls, flirting with the women in their summer dresses. Thompson knew better. He knew how these people sugar-gummed you to your face; then later, after the ax fell, treated you with the same compunction they would a turkey at the evening table.

Lieutenant Mann's eyes drifted over to the suitcase, then to Thompson.

"I'm here in regards to the Lombard murder. You've heard about it, I'm sure."

"In the paper."

"You were acquainted with Mr. Lombard?"

"That's true."

"When was the last time you saw him?"

"Last night, down at Musso's."

"What did you talk about?"

"We didn't speak. I only saw him from across the room."

The lieutenant considered this and went on considering. He gandered once more at the suitcase. He held his white hat in his lap, running his fingers around its brim.

"We've been talking to a lot of people. People say things, as I am sure you know, and from what I hear. . ."

Thompson cut him off. Maybe Lieutenant Mann here was a bumpkin, or maybe it was just a routine, but Thompson didn't mean to play this game. "I'm not the only person who had trouble with Lombard. He screwed people right and left."

"So I've heard."

Thompson felt the heat under his collar. He was sweating. I should be quiet, he told himself. This cop is nothing but a country clown and here I am. . .

"When was the last time you were at his house?"

"Never."

"How about last night? Where were you?"

The cop set his hat aside. His manner was still boyish. He sat with his hands together, resting between his knees, his hair greased up pretty well, though not well enough to control his cowlick. A shank of black hair stuck straight up. At the moment, Lieutenant Mann didn't look so much like a cop as he did a preacher's son, the kind of kid who spent his days nailing up loose boards around the chapel.

"I was at home," Thompson lied.

"Here?"

"No."

"Where?"

"At the Ardmore penthouse. With my wife."

Mann chewed on that. "Alberta?" he asked.

"Yes."

Thompson felt a quiver in his knees. If Mann knew Alberta's name, perhaps he'd been up to see her. If so, the cop likely knew his alibi was a lie.

"Let me ask you something," said the cop. "I got a chance to look at some of those books of yours. And I been wondering. They got much biography in them? Auto, I mean. Tales of the self." Thompson looked at him blankly. The cop's face was guileless as the moon. "I mean, you seem like a nice guy. And I ask myself, how could a nice guy write books like those. I tell myself, well, all of us, we got something a little weird inside. I say, okay, so it's there inside him too. Then I wonder, what is it like? You know, to be thinking those kind of things you think. A man up to his neck in a pile of shit. A women cutting off her husband's privates with a piece of glass. A man hitting his girlfriend with his fist. In the gut. Hitting her so hard her stomach busts. That blood bursts out her mouth like some kind of star exploding between her teeth. It makes me wonder."

"About what?"

"Well us cops, we see so much stuff sometimes. We walk so close to the edge, sometimes a man crosses over. For example, a vice man, undercover. After a while he isn't undercover anymore. He's just under. He's not just watching. He's part of the show."

"I see."

"So don't you ever worry, the things you write, just describing things like that, back there in the recesses, about what might happen? You contemplate a thing long enough, you describe it—you make it part of the world. And some things, maybe they should be left alone."

Thompson didn't have an answer. Though he didn't want to admit it, he'd wondered the same thing himself, a time or two. That voice inside, though, it was hard to deny. You could try for a little while, maybe. Walk over to the shelf, uncork the bottle—but then a whole new batch of demons came flying out.

"You were working on a project with Mr. Lombard?" asked Mann.

"Yes. But the status now—it's kind of murky."

Mann wandered over to the window, studied the street. From his angle, Thompson could see out too. The street was pretty much empty, except for a young man on crutches, thin and scraggly. The guy looked as if he had just walked across the desert on those crutches. Thompson expected the cop to ask him more about his relationship with Lombard, but instead he just stood there, studying the cripple.

"Why do you do it?" Mann asked at last.

Thompson felt a bit of panic, as if he were being accused of the murder. Then he realized the cop was asking about his writing again.

"It's my talent," Thompson said. "And I get paid."

"What does your wife think about it?"

"She likes it."

"You sure?"

Thompson hesitated. "Yeah."

Mann waited at the window. The young man had been joined by a woman now. On crutches too. Heavy as the man was thin, twice as battered. They hobbled together down the street.

"It takes all kinds to make a world." Mann nodded in the way country people do at such expressions, as if he had just said something original. There was a gleam in his eye, though. "You know how they say, a lid for every pot."

"Sure," Thompson said. The cop was a cornponing him, but he had no choice but to play along. "A kettle for every stove."

"That's right. And a match for every fire."

Then Lieutenant Mann stood up, his hat in his hand. He seemed finished, as if he'd gotten what he needed, though in fact Thompson couldn't see how he'd gotten much at all.

"You got any leads?"

Something imperceptible shifted in the cop's face, and Thompson regretted the question. It was the kind of thing a guilty man might ask, looking to see how much the cops knew.

"A few. Objects at the crime scene. Maybe the killer left them behind, maybe not."

"Oh."

Thompson recalled his missing shoe, his wallet, and saw at the same time how Lieutenant Mann studied his face. He nodded at Thompson's suitcase.

"You going somewhere."

"No."

"That's good," the cop said. "Now you take care. And good luck with your writing."

Mann tipped his hat and left. Thompson listened to the cop's footsteps fade down the hall. His own shirt was soaked through with sweat. The heat. He slammed down a drink. Stripped off his shirt. Trapped. The cops on one side. Miracle on the other. He shook his head. Mann did not know anything, not yet. Just blowing smoke up a hole.

Another knock—and Thompson about leaped from his skin.

"Who's there?"

"Courier."

Thompson remembered. He'd called the Studio

Courier. He swung the door open and handed the boy his message for Lussie. The courier was a blue-eyed kid who aspired to stardom, no doubt, but in the meantime it was his job to drive envelopes around town.

When the kid was gone, Thompson poured himself another drink. He stripped off the rest of his clothes and lay buck-naked on the bed, an old man sweating in the Hollywood heat.

NINETEEN

THOMPSON THOUGHT ABOUT LUSSIE. He felt that old tremble, smelling for an instant that heavy green smell he used to smell in the night air in Lincoln, when he stood on her porch and the yellow light was on her (or maybe it had been Alberta under the porch light; his memory confused things). She wore a farm girl dress, scooped at the neck, so you could see her collarbone. Up close to her like that, it had seemed he could smell the night even thicker around them both, along with the soap on her body that could not hide, not completely, her animal smell.

They had gone for a walk, up the hill behind her house, and Lussie was all innocence in her cotton dress.

"What are you thinking about?" she asked. "What's really inside you?"

He looked down at the lights of the little village, and heard the sound of some cow lowing, children playing by the river. All that stuff is in me, he wanted to say, the whole business—but something else, too, an undercurrent in his head like the undercurrent in the Platte, washing things to shore. Old boots, maybe; a bullwhip; a petticoat stained with blood.

She pulled away, tightening her knees, and would not let him kiss her.

Years later, when they met in New York, things had changed. Something different in her eyes. They had a few drinks in her hotel room, and she leaned sloppily against the wall, innocence gone, a bit of the matron in her hips. He touched her cheek. That was the moment, then. His chance. Blue flecks in her glimmering eyes. Instead, he went out into the hall. More ice. By the time he returned, she'd recovered herself. They went to the bar in the lobby. Somc fricnds of hers happened along, fellow travelers, and the evening was finished.

He climbed out of bed and got dressed. Slipped on his white jacket. Outside, he bought a bouquet of flowers and strung a carnation through his lapel.

He wondered if she would appear.

Inside Musso's, he ordered himself a double shot and waited. He lounged. He watched the door. Soon it was six clock. Then it was six thirty. He sipped. Time passed. When the door next opened, the person who stepped through was not Lussie. Rather it was Billy Miracle. A step or two behind, entering the bar with the air of a bereaved widow, was Michele Haze.

TWENTY

UNDER THE NEW CIRCUMSTANCES, Haze and Miracle carried about them an aura of intense glamour. It was the glamour of death, visceral and irresistible, and it had its own smell, its own way of hushing a room. It had too its own hue and texture, a distinct means of coloring the light, electrifying the air.

Miracle surveyed the Musso & Frank Grill with an odd grandeur. He placed a hand on Michele's forearm. Something in his demeanor—solicitous on one hand, proprietary on the other—reminded him of those men who accompany famous widows down the aisle at the funerals of their recently slain husbands.

He let loose and came toward Thompson.

"The other night, you get home all right?"

"Sure. I got home."

"Hell, you were a walking blackout. A raging beast. It's a wonder you remember anything."

"I remember fine," Thompson lied.

"We tried dropping you off at your place. Up to the Ardmore. But you, hell. You wouldn't even get out of the car. You wanted to see Jack. Over and over, you yelled. 'I want to see Jack.'"

Thompson looked away.

"No? We tried to humor you, all the way down Sunset. You got out of the car on the Plaza. We wrestled you back in, but then you pulled the same stunt further down the road. You just bolted. Down around Beverly Drive. The last I saw, you were ambling up toward the hills."

Miracle smiled with unrestrained pleasure. Thompson didn't like the implications, because the producer's story put him headed toward Lombard's the night of the murder. He wondered if Billy had told the same thing to the police. If that story was the reason Mann had stopped by his place at the Aztec.

Meanwhile, Michele Haze stood by the bar, all in black, waiting for a drink. Some industry somebody was consoling her, putting his hands on her shoulders, brushing his lips across her cheeks, letting his fingers linger sadly, reassuringly, on her blouse, her velvet skirt.

"Jack's death," said Miracle, "it leaves a great void. A spiritual absence."

"Is it going to affect our deal?"

Miracle laughed. "That's what I like about you, Jimbo. You just come out with it. But Lombard wasn't such a bad guy. He had his flaws but hey, it's a tough industry. Shark eat shark. And he made some great pictures."

Thompson glanced again towards Michelle Haze. The industry somebody was gone, but another had taken his place—and a third waited in the wings.

"Let's get down to business. About the book you're doing for me, my thought is this. It's time to pick up the pace. You got the killer in Texas, dilly-dallying with these two women. The good girl, the bad girl. As fascinating as that is, well, I think it's time for the drifter to finish his business in Texas and move on."

"Where do you want him?" Thompson was relieved, in a way, to get to the business of the story.

"Get him here. To Los Angeles. That's what *The Manifesto* is all about. The siren call."

"I don't follow."

"The voice inside the brain, Jimbo. The one that begs for murder, you know what I mean."

It was the way Miracle worked, Thompson knew. In his films, the producer borrowed bits and pieces from the stories of real-life hoodlums, and from the lives of Hollywood celebrities, too, and merged them together on-screen.

"Well, your man in Texas, he hears that voice. He listens to it, and it leads him here. All the way to Los Angeles."

"What happens then?"

Miracle leaned over the table.

"We've been through this. He's given a contract. For murder."

"Who does he kill?"

"A Hollywood starlet," said Miracle. "The third wheel, remember. The other girl in the triangle."

Thompson felt a chill. The story Miracle described had a familiar resonance. The dead girl. Lombard. Michele Haze.

"The point here," said Miracle, "is that the killer, he's not his own man. He's created by the people who need him. Me, you, the audience. It's a collaborative effort."

Miracle eyes held an unruly light. On the surface, he seemed to be in control. He had a plan, and he was working it through. Except there was something wrong: a crooked line on the blueprint, a screwy bit of thinking. (It happened often enough, Thompson knew. People cracked. Maybe the screwiness wasn't in their heads, or had not been there to begin with anyway. Maybe it came from on high, from some boss somewhere, who in turn had another boss of his own, with another boss behind him. It made for a crazed look in the eye, trying to serve the wishes of some remote master, some invisible son-of-a-bitch.)

Maybe that's what had happened, Thompson figured. Miracle was getting pressure from his gangland buddy, and he'd gone over the edge.

Michele Haze left the bar now. Her consolers had done with her. They were satiated, filled with the smell of her, done patting and touching.

"Sit down, sweetie," said Miracle.

She held herself with a certain elegance, glassy-eyed, serene in her grief. Since the other night, slumped in the town car, she had regained her composure.

The door behind them opened. Thompson turned.

Lussie Jones.

I shouldn't have chosen this place. Someplace else, maybe, not here.

He peered toward the door. Behind her, the late afternoon sun glowered over the broken rooftops, and the woman stood like a shadow in the light, a familiar figure, but he couldn't make out the features the way she stood, the light falling so harsh behind her. Then the door fell shut.

His heart beat more quickly. The woman standing there was not Lussie Jones. It was Alberta.

Dearest wife.

She stood poised in the doorway. She had dolled herself up, so standing there like she did, she looked pretty good.

Her gray hair was cut blunt. She had done her lips with a faint gloss and put a strand of pearls around her collar. Up close, he could see the freckles where her blouse opened, and he could smell too the blue lilac smell that she had possessed even when she was young and spread her legs for him on an oversprung mattress in a roadside joint somewhere in Nebraska.

"Why are you here?"

"Just getting out of the house."

"How did you know where I'd be?"

"It doesn't take a genius. You came and got your suitcase?"

"Yeah."

"Why?"

"Franny's out of town, and her place, in La Jolla, it's empty. I thought I'd go down and get some work done."

"I see."

At the table, the flowers for Lussie lay on the empty seat. He hustled the bouquet aside, but Alberta noticed, and her suspicions were aroused. She gave Michele Haze the old up and down, but he could see, too, that she did not think a movie star like her would have much to do with the likes of him.

"When are you going?" she asked.

Thompson shrugged, not wanting to talk about his future whereabouts in front of Miracle. Alberta went on regardless. "Jimmy's got himself a room down at the Aztec Hotel. He's always done that, ever since we were married. He gets an assignment and he's out of the house."

Miracle nodded.

"Now, he's going down to LaJolla for a few days. To his sister's house. Though Lord knows, the car won't budge. And why he would need to wear his white suit coat, that's a question I can't answer." Alberta laughed. She held her hand to her throat. "Or why, indeed, he would need flowers for the trip!"

"I bought them for you."

"But Jimmy, you didn't know I was coming here."

He had no response.

Michele leaned into the conversation. Her lips were unnaturally red, her cheeks pale. She feathered the air with her hands as she spoke. "Jim was just saying, before you came. He meant to bring you flowers as a surprise."

It was a lie, spoken softly. Michele glanced his way, and he saw her face as it had been the moment before she and Miracle had let him go, dropping him into the abyss. There was something else in her expression, though, a note of pleading—as if she needed something, wanted his help.

The moment ended, and the bartender strolled dutifully to their table.

"Phone call," he said. "For Jim Thompson."

•

"Hello?"

"Jim?"

"Yes."

"This is Lucille."

"Lussie?"

"Yes."

Her voice was matter-of-fact as the kitchen table, a little bit sweet but nasal too, impossible to read. The perfect surface, you could not know what lay beneath it. Meanwhile Alberta watched from across the room.

"I would love to meet with you, but I'm tied up this evening. And Walter, my husband, he gets in day after tomorrow. There's this dance the following evening. The Dentistry Association Ball," she laughed, self-deprecating, almost. He could not tell what that laughter might mean.

"I understand." He turned his back on Alberta, but it did no good. "How much longer you going to be in town?"

"Till the end of the week."

"I'd love to see you. Talk over old times."

She laughed again.

"I have a place out near La Jolla. I'll be there tomorrow night."

"Jim. . ."

"If you want to visit, just come. We can talk."

"Will Alberta be there?"

He glanced toward his wife, but she had turned from him now, and was chatting nervously with Miracle and Haze.

"No. Alberta won't be there."

She hesitated. "I'll try," she said.

"You try."

They talked a little longer. Then he gave her his sister's phone number, and got off the line.

"Who was that?" Alberta asked

"My agent," he lied.

"Alberta was just telling us about your dad," said Miracle. "He was a lawman, back in Oklahoma?"

"A long time ago."

"Jimmy's still got the pistol, don't you honey?"

"Yes. Just a souvenir."

"In fact, you brought it with you down to that hotel, didn't you? For protection."

"It's good luck. That's why I keep it." The conversation was going off in too many directions. "So our deal's still on," he asked Miracle, "you want me to finish *The Manifesto*?"

"I don't see why not. We have a contract, don't we?"

"That's right. We have a contract."

•

Later, Thompson held the door open for Alberta, and they went together out onto the street. She was wearing her heels, looking smart. It was dusk, and the boulevard had some of its old glamour, as if glitter were falling from the sky.

"You got yourself dressed up. Your white coat."

"A man has to have some self-respect."

"Especially when he means to surprise his wife." Her

voice held the slightest edge. "Bringing me flowers. How sweet!"

"That's right. Let me escort you home."

He hailed a taxi and slid in beside her. It was only a few blocks, but Alberta did not like walking in Hollywood. Little things like this had run them broke. He didn't care. He liked riding above the sidewalk, like some kind of big shot. He sidled up close to her and put his hand on her leg, and he began to feel like it was 40 years ago, and she was just a young woman. Impressed with the young man who'd shown up on her porch, slouching and muttering and just the faintest bit drunk. He gave her a kiss in the backseat now (thinking of Lussie, that hillside long ago, the hotel room in New York), and Alberta kissed him a little too, putting her hands on his crotch. He was sixty-four years old, but he liked it, and imagined he always would. The taxi pulled up in front of the apartment, and suddenly he wanted up into that penthouse. He wanted to go up there with her. Alberta put a hand on his chest and pushed him back into the taxi.

"Not tonight, buddy."

The taxi took him back down the street. He got off on Sunset, with an erection stirring in his pants.

He wondered why Alberta had come down to Musso's, only to push him way, but the answer wasn't hard to see. She was angry and she wasn't going to let him off the hook, not so easy, after all these years.

Meantime, he was bulging at the seams, or close enough, anyway, for a man of his years. He touched himself in the street, keeping the hard-on alive, then walked into Hollywood Liquors for a pint. He shoved the pint in his front hip pocket, right there next to his erection, and sauntered on home. In the old days, these streets had been full of cream-skinned beauties and movie palaces, and the air had smelled of desert sage. Maybe, but it wasn't true anymore. The streets were full of hopheads and pot smokers and gutter trash from around the world. He wouldn't have looked at them twice—the latest fashion in riff-raff, scum of the moment, pigs du jour—except he feared what might emerge from the crowd. The Oklahoman. That son-of-bitch who had dropped that Cadillac outside his apartment, with the dead girl in the trunk.

Pops, I want to talk to you.

His erection faded. Some kids hooted at him, laughing just because he was old. He knew how he must look out here in the hard light, under the neon. The ugliness of his face, the savage wrinkles, the puckered mouth. He lit a cigarette, and felt the smoke curl from his lips. Hideous smoke, it tasted like crap. I am ugly, all right, and for an instant he was proud of his ugliness, then he began to cough, hacking, and the cough dredged up the yellow scum in his lungs and he spat the scum onto the sidewalk. Even the whores looked at him in disgust. No wonder my wife won't touch me, he thought, but it isn't my fault. A person gets uglier, and more disgusting, just walking down these streets.

•

Inside the hotel, the clerk sat behind the front desk, fast asleep in his faded monkey outfit. He leaned back in his chair, eyes closed, his hands folded together, like a Cossack sleeping at his post.

Thompson sat awhile in the lobby, watching the kid sleep. He took a drink, then another, and felt himself getting angry. Ignoramus, he thought. You don't know what's out there waiting for you, kiddo. Clever business associates. A wife that won't touch you. A corpse on every corner—and an old man's cock that swells up when you're not looking, and disappears as soon as you touch it.

Thompson stood close. The desk clerk didn't mind him. He slept like a baby. Little fuck. Innocent little bastard. I knew a kid like you once.

Thompson sucked on his Pall Mall. On the spur of the moment, overcome by meanness, he put the cigarette on the boy's uniform, where the arms made a cradle, and watched it roll, disappearing into the thick folds. In a minute or two it would burn through the coat, burn the fuck out of the boy, but by that time Thompson would be upstairs and the kid wouldn't know what hit him.

TWENTY-ONE

THAT NIGHT, THOMPSON woke up coughing. In his dreams, he had seen his father. Big Jim Thompson, gunslinger, wildcat oil man, friend of W. D. Harding and every racketeer in the West. All of those things were true about his father, more or less. In his heyday, Big Jim had been sheriff of Anadarko, in the badlands of Oklahoma. He'd been a popular sheriff, a back-slapper, a preserver of the common interest and enemy of hooligans. Or that's the way it had seemed until he was forced to resign over financial shortages at the jail.

The old man turned to wildcatting. In his letters home there was always the promise of money, a big strike any day now.

Soon, it was the son's turn to be Big Jim Thompson, to ride his thumb into the oil fields and find himself a job. He sent money home to his mom and his sister, but the fields wore him down. He tried college. He met Alberta. After he was married, mom and sis moved in. Later, he moved the whole bunch out to California. Meanwhile, his father drifted the Midwest. The circle of the old man's wandering grew smaller and smaller, until he paced the yard of an old folks home in Nebraska, and then one day word came that Big Jim had choked to death on the excelsior from his mattress.

Thompson coughed. He poured himself a drink. He plunged into a black sleep in which it was impossible to tell the difference between himself and his father, between the life he imagined and the one he had lived. The world got blacker with every step, round a corner of brick and slanted light, down an alley where every side door had its lamp burned out and behind those doors were alleys where the air was darker still.

A woman leaned toward him. Her tongue inside his mouth was rough and papery.

"More," she whispered.

He couldn't see her face. He tried to pull away, but she held him fast, and he put his hand against her throat.

"More," she insisted.

She pushed him away, pulled him close, both at the same time. The blackness grew yet blacker. He could not move.

He awoke. For a moment, his arms would not respond, nor his legs. Finally, he staggered up, his arm was numb, there was blood on his pillow. He looked in the mirror, and there was more blood on his face.

The doctor had warned him. You keep it up, the way you're living, you'll hemorrhage, buddy, you'll have yourself a stroke.

He dressed slowly. Just a nosebleed, he told himself. Everything'll be all right, soon as I get out of town. He buttoned his shirt, hoisted up his suitcase with his good arm, then stumbled into the harlot streets.

TWENTY-TWO

THOMPSON HAILED A TAXI to the Santa Monica station, then took a Greyhound down the Pacific Coast Highway. Outside, there was that white sun and that white sand and that white sky full of salt and the strangled call of gulls. When you looked at the combers through the bus windows—in their gauze blouses and bright shorts, their Raybans and polo shirts—they all seemed aloof and unknowable, as if they moved in a secret and pure realm that left their heads full of light. When these same people strolled inside the bus, though, it was a different story. You could see the desire in their faces, too, and smell the sweat and the lotion, hear the grunts and see the struggle of the body to make itself comfortable, and notice too the flaws in the features, the jaws that were too sharp, the heads that came to a point, the breasts that sagged and the bellies that drooped. They lost their aura, here in the bus. They became like him, leaning their heads back into the cushion, watching the scenery in the tinted glass.

Finally, he arrived in La Jolla. His sister had a cottage off the main street. He dallied in the kitchen, thinking about Lussie Jones, wondering if she would call. Then he set up his typewriter. It was why he had come. To escape the situation. To finish his assignment and be done.

> I was trapped. It was the old two way pull, and I didn't know which way to go.
>
> By day, it was Gloria, tugging sweetly at my hand. By night, it was her sister, twisting between the sheets.
>
> The old two-hearted tug, I knew

all about it. My momma, I use to follow her legs with my eyes, right up to where they disappeared into one another, and I knew how those men felt when they looked at her. I wished I didn't know. Because it wasn't how a boy was supposed to feel. And a mom wasn't supposed to laugh at her son, either, the way she laughed at me, seeing that look in my eyes.

Now I wanted things simple. Pure. With Gloria, it could be what way, I thought.

But Belle, she'd found out about my past somehow. She was on to me. "You be nice," she said. "You do as I say." And she let me know that my plans, whatever they might be, were going to take a back seat to hers. Or else.

Then one afternoon, she sent me down to the druggist to pick up a prescription for her father. I should have known. I'd seen her and the druggist together. I should have guessed—but I didn't. I delivered the medicine.

A few hours later I knocked on Daddy Lanier's office door.

No one answered.

"Sir," I said

I pushed it open.

Inside, Daddy Lanier sat slumped over his desk, head down, cheek pressed to the wood. In his hand, he clutched the prescription bottle.

He was dead.

And me—I wasn't wise enough yet to see who'd get the blame.

Late that evening, a car drove by. It rolled past slowly, and the light from its head lamps wheeled across the kitchen walls.

The driver cut the motor, and Thompson listened for the car door. When the sound didn't come, he peered out the window. The car stood in the blue fog halfway down the block.

Who could it be?

Lussie. Or perhaps Lieutenant Mann had had him followed.

Thompson dropped the curtain. A shadow had moved inside the car, he thought, but he could not be sure. He slopped two fingers worth into one of his sister's jelly glasses, and listened for the sound of footsteps on the walk. They didn't come. Then the phone rang.

"Jim Thompson?" a woman asked—but it wasn't the voice he expected. Rather, it belonged to Michele Haze.

She had remembered Alberta mentioning La Jolla, she explained, and his sister's name. With that much, she had dialed information.

"I need to meet with you."

"Tonight?"

"There's a place on the highway down there. The Pacific Café. It's open late."

Thompson knew the place. On the bluff, above the ocean. The owner had decorated the walls with publicity shots. Glossies everywhere, every star there had ever been. Thompson picked up the curtain and took another glimmer out. The car sat as before.

It was late, he told himself. If Lussie meant to come, she'd be here by now.

"Will you meet me?" Michele asked

He closed his eyes and let the dice roll in his head.

"All right."

TWENTY-THREE

THOMPSON SCUTTLED DOWN the alley behind his sister's house. He moved faster than he thought he could, like an old crab startled out of its shell. The alley opened onto a side street—empty and dark except for a traffic signal at the corner. On the other side of the highway, the Pacific Café slumped out over the bluff. As he crossed the road, he heard the neon hissing in its blue sign. The fog had lifted along the coast, and the black sea glistened like oil on the beach below.

Inside, the owner had kept up the old decor. The walls were plastered with the photos, and there was a shot of Michele Haze, taken a couple of decades before, in her starlet years, young and vampish. Her eyes had the sleepy sheen that had made her famous, and she held her lips in the same cashmere pout. She had built her career around that glance, and the soft, almost drunken lisp with which she spoke.

A white limo pulled into the lot, and Thompson watched the chauffeur saunter up the walk.

"Michele will talk to you. Inside the car."

Thompson found Michele in the limousine, waiting for him, just like the chauffeur said. She wore straight slacks and a cotton shirt and a scarf over her platinum hair. No make-up, her clothes rumpled and mussed. She gave him a shrug—and her eyes were for an instant the same eyes as those of the picture inside, no difference in the world.

"To what do I owe this privilege?"

"I felt you should know some things. There's not going to be any movie."

"What do you mean?"

"Jack never signed. There's no deal."

The news did not surprise him. He had suspected the deal was falling apart.

Her eyes grew misty.

"The girl. Jack didn't have her out of his system. She disappeared on him, and I thought maybe he was done with her. Soon as I saw him, that last time in Musso's, I knew I was wrong. He was going back to her. He was going to kill the picture, and leave me behind."

Michele shrugged again, fatalistic. After all, she knew how these things went. She'd been a Young Lovely once herself.

"He told Billy to drop dead. That he would never work with him in a million years."

Thompson remembered that evening at Musso's, a few days before, when it all happened, how Lombard had left, and Miracle had gone barrelling after him.

"I waited for them to come back. Somehow, part of me, I thought maybe Jack, that he would change his mind again. That he might still come back to Musso's that night."

"How long did you wait?"

"An hour, maybe. An hour-and-a-half. But Jack didn't come back. Only Billy, alone."

"Did Billy catch up with Jack? Did they talk?"

She didn't respond, but he knew the answer. Or what she wanted him to think. It was there, unspoken, in the blue neon that flickered and fell over the white limousine and its tinted windows to make indecipherable shadows on her face. Miracle had followed Lombard up to his house. Up there, alone, he had gone berserk and when he was done, he'd washed his hands and his face and wiped the blood off his shoes and driven on down to Musso's. Then he'd decided to frame up old Jim Thompson. Put a little dope in the old man's drink and drag him back to the scene of the crime.

"You helped him."

"No, I loved Jack."

"You doped me. You dragged me up there, the two of you."

"I didn't have any choice."

She closed her eyes. The dope—Miracle had gotten it out of her purse he figured, fumbling around on the seat. It was the source of her sleepy eyes, that languor in front of the camera. There had been a time before all that he guessed—when she'd been just some kid in somebody's hometown, the girl next door who just had to get out. Leaving behind a mom and a pop and a boy in a pick up truck.

"Did you hire the Okie?"

"What do you mean?"

"You were jealous of the girl, and now she's dead. The Okie killed her, didn't he?"

She didn't answer but instead glanced toward the café and he imagined she was thinking about the girl in the picture on the wall inside.

"That's what Miracle holds over you. That's why you have to go along with him."

"No, Billy arranged it. He had her killed."

"Why would he do that?"

"He was convinced, if The Young Lovely was gone, he could persuade Jack to do the picture."

"He told you this?"

"Before it happened, I thought he was joking. I didn't think he'd actually go ahead. . . If you help me, I'll go to the police. I'll tell them what happened that night at Lombard's house. I'll tell them who the real murderer was. I just need you to do something first. Contact somebody for me."

Thompson said nothing. She paused, trying to read his face. For his part, he wondered how much to believe.

"Billy had someone else arrange it, the girl's death," she said. "And that man, he hired the Okie to do the job. Only Billy didn't pay up—and now the Okie is after me."

"Why you?"

"When Billy set up her murder, he gave them my name. So now I have to pay off to get rid of them. Once I'm free of them, I can talk to the cops. I'll tell them you didn't have anything to do with this."

"I don't know. This type of thing. A guy like me, my age. Chasing someone down."

"The contact man—the one who arranged the murder. If you could set up a meeting with him. Tell him I'll pay."

She gave Thompson a hopeless look. He thought again of that starlet in the picture inside the cafe, and he realized he'd been wrong before. There was a difference. Back then, she'd just been posing. She'd been somebody else, pretending to be this woman in the picture, desperate, glamorous. Now the pretense was gone—but it wasn't just that. Michele brushed a hand against his leg, and in the flickering neon her face had the look of a translucent doll.

Fear, he decided, that was it. The different thing in her eyes.

"What's the man's name? The contact?"

"Wicks. Sydney Wicks."

Thompson felt his skin bristle.

"In East Hollywood," she pleaded. "A place called the Satellite Bar."

TWENTY-FOUR

That night I went over to the Lanier place, but Gloria was out, making arrangement for her Daddy's funeral. I let myself in, and all but stumbled across Belle in the darkened parlor. I held back, though, and saw her take a man's face between her hands. They kissed, the pharmacist and Belle. They talked it up big. About how it was going to be when the will was cashed out and Belle had gotten her father's money.

I listened to them for awhile, and at last I realized. They'd poisoned the old man and planned to pin the whole business on me. As if I'd tampered with the medicine.

I switched on the light and Belle's eyes went wide. She tried to explain her way out of it, but I already had Daddy Lanier's pistol in my hand. I knew, soon as they autopsied the old man, the sheriff would be coming for me. Given who I was, no one would believe my story, I knew that too. My only chance was to get out of town. I had to buy time. So I took two chairs from the dinner table and strung them together.

"Please," pleaded Belle. "My neck."

I gave the cord an extra pull and stuffed a rag in her mouth. I did the same for the druggist.

Something inside told me I should do this differently. With Gloria's help, maybe, and a good lawyer, I could get out clean. After all I hadn't killed anybody. They were the ones. Even so, there was another, older voice inside me.

You dope, boy, you goddamn fool.

I headed toward that voice now. There was an old man, an ex-con out in California, who'd told me if I ever got myself in a fix, come see him. I drove. Somewhere in the desert, the next day, the news came over the radio. A man and a woman had been found dead in a central Texas living room. The pair had tried to free themselves, twisting and squirming, but each movement had only brought the cord tighter about their necks.

TWENTY-FIVE

THOMPSON COULDN'T SLEEP. Instead he kept writing. He pictured the drifter coming down the Barstow grade into California, the desert streaming past in the black of night, then the slow bloom of suburban lights. The air whispered through the windwings of the Cadillac, and Thompson could see the drifter's lips moving as he thought about Belle and the druggist, the rope tight around their necks. Thompson's lips moved too. Soon the man was over the hills and into the Los Angeles basin.

Thompson tore the sheet from his typewriter.

He did not like what was happening. He'd written *The Manifesto* based on what Miracle had given him. Now, the character he'd created was in Los Angeles.

That first night in Musso's, Miracle had laid out the story. The drifter in Texas. The love triangle in Los Angeles. The dead girl.

Now that story was coming true. Haze, Lombard, The Young Lovely—they were the triangle. The Okie was the drifter.

"Why me?" Thompson asked himself. "Why did Miracle get me involved?"

I'm the fall guy. The stumblebum. Someone to blame when things go wrong.

Also, Miracle had needed a writer.

There was something flawed in the plan: the notion you could arrange a murder, then make a movie about it, place the blame elsewhere. Producers, though, guys like Miracle, they thought they ran the world. Or liked to think so. Put a spoon to their nose, well, things could get pretty skewed.

Even so, things were not converging the way Miracle had planned. The Okie had lost the corpse. So Miracle had improvised. And now Lombard was dead too.

Thompson almost sympathized. He'd been up against that wall himself, clutching all those ragged ends, stories within stories that almost webbed together, the various pieces fraying and disappearing into a darkness that swallowed all calculation. Meanwhile, the killer you had created roamed the city. Your careful plan—out of control.

•

It was dawn. The sedan out front had not moved. A green sedan, Thompson saw now, in the first light of morning. It had a familiar look, and no longer seemed frightening. If someone had meant to harm him, they'd had all night.

Thompson stepped outside.

A figure slumped on the driver's side, head against the window. He edged closer. A woman. She stretched her arms, waking up—and he saw who it was, and he was surprised, though perhaps he shouldn't have been. She had tracked him down, just as she had tracked him down at Musso's night before last. The sedan, he recognized it now. It belonged to their neighbor, Mrs. Myers.

"Alberta?"

She blushed. "I decided to come pay you a visit."

"When?"

"This morning, of course. I just got here."

She was lying, of course. She had borrowed the car yesterday, he guessed, and been parked out there all night, though she would never admit it.

"You want to come in for some breakfast?"

"Thank you."

It was Sunday morning, and he remembered the sound of the kids rumbling about in the front room long ago, roughhousing, and he remembered Alberta watching from the table, still young, smelling of sleep and a midnight tumble.

"Do you remember when we first met?" she asked.

"Yeah."

"Some college party. You were drinking a beer—and I liked the way you held the bottle to your lips."

"That's right."

"Yes—but I didn't know you were going to be holding it there for the next forty years."

The night they'd met, he'd seen her leaning against the wall in her red blouse and black slacks. She'd been watching him. The other young men there, they'd smelled of the farm. Young Jim Thompson, though, he'd been around. Debonair, sauntering, reckless, his shirt collar unbuttoned and his tie loose. He'd had experiences. The only loose plank in a room of stiff boards. Their first date, they went to a gangster movie. He had gotten his hands under her blouse, unbuttoning her skirt band. Her features one moment had the look of innocence, and the next seemed as sharp and wicked as a fence post dipped in tetanus.

"How are our kids?" he asked.

"Fine."

It was an odd question, a sore point. His daughters had married and moved away, but their son, well, he took after the old man. He liked the bar room.

Thompson cracked the eggs into the pan now, flipped the sunny sides over without breaking them.

"They're coming up perfect."

"You could always cook an egg."

He got the breakfast onto the table, and they sat together reading the paper. They slipped into the old routine, and he saw the age in her face. She had on her white blouse, rumpled from the long night in the car, her skirt that flared at the bottom, white hose, black pumps, a string of pearls. Her nails were painted red. She had been spying on him, out there. She'd come prepared to drag him from the arms of another woman, if need be, but at the same time she meant to look good doing it.

"Why don't you give it up?"

"What?"

His eyes followed hers, and he saw the bottle that stood on the coffee table. It wasn't just the booze, she would say. He knew the argument. It's the whole thing, Jim, the whole business. You pretend it's for me, but the penthouse—you're the one who wanted it, honey, Jim. All I've ever wanted was something simple and clean. A little place with a flower box in the window where the light shines through. And if it all isn't quite what I imagine, I'm willing to pretend. So long as my husband doesn't keep plummeting down that long staircase into the dark.

That was her argument. Thompson knew it, without her saying a word, just like she knew his response. You wanted that penthouse, Birdie. And hell, when it comes to that staircase, you're the one taking me by the hand, pushing me down.

"You've done things the way you wanted. You've written your books."

"I know."

"That new place, it isn't so awful."

"Yeah it is."

"Go back to your work."

She stood up. She was gorgeous, his wife. He didn't want her to leave. She was all but finished with him, though, ready to give him the push over, the way a person got after spending all night in the car.

"I have to go."

"I'll be back Friday. To help with the move."

She turned away, and he saw the arch of the young girl's back, the housewife's tits, the tired legs of an old woman whose skirt ended at the dimple in her knees. She was all these women at once. They were all masks, the dust amusing itself.

"Good-bye."

It was the Oklahoma voice again. The voice of his mother, his sisters. Of the front porch swing creaking in the back of their throats. In it, he could hear the cicadas, and the katydids and the hollering moan of some old yellow dog. Then his wife was gone out the door, and Thompson felt a pang in his heart. He gathered up all his papers and hurried after.

"Take me back to the city."

They rode together. Past the orange groves and the oil derricks and the Long Beach shipyards. Up the winding coast and over the flats into Anaheim. Then over the Santa Monica cloverleaf where you glimpsed it all at once—or thought you did—all those streets, Wilshire, and Pico and Lincoln, running parallel to each other and away, coming back and crossing. Spiraling towards the center but still always on the rim. Bunker Hill, Hollywood, Chinatown, Burbank. One long town with one long street. Stucco houses under a white sun that spun around other suns in a galaxy inside a universe black as black could be.

Alberta didn't take him with her back to their place at the Ardmore. If he had asked, maybe, but she had her pride.

She pulled over on Hollywood Boulevard, not far from the Aztec. Lussie had not shown up at his sister's place, Michele Haze wanted him to find Sydney Wicks at the Satellite Bar, his book was unfinished. Still, he couldn't care about those things now. He reached over to kiss his wife. She responded, almost. He put his hand on her belt, where the white blouse disappeared into her skirt, and placed his lips on her cheeks. She closed her eyes and let him have the corner of her lips.

He considered giving her the money inside the envelope. Like she said, though, it wasn't enough, and he still had a vision of himself snaking away, leaving this all behind, slipping over the border into some foreign country where volcanoes rumbled up out of nothing and the senoritas danced in the shadows, naked, voluptuous, full of piss, full of life.

TWENTY-SIX

SHE DROPPED HIM AT THE CORNER, a block from the hotel. It was a long block, a hard bit of sidewalk. He walked with the manuscript tucked underneath one arm, his suitcase under the other, all the time worrying it would slip from his fingers. The feeling in his arm hadn't come back all the way, not yet.

An old son of a bitch spat on the street in front of him. A whore farted and belched, mocking Thompson as he passed. Across the way two long-haired idiots passed a pipe back and forth, and a young woman clutched at herself, teeth clattering, hands shaking, as if she were about to jump out of her skin.

This is it. Where I belong, he thought. Walking the blind alleys where there's a song of gloom behind every eyelid. In the good old days, I was a hophead with the best of them. Vitamin shots and transfusions and anything else that a gave a jolt to the nervous system. These days he settled for the simple stuff. Bought himself a bottle at the corner and went inside the hotel.

`. . . into a dark room where the shades were drawn and the only light was that which fell in a harsh slant through the blinds. In that light I didn't see him as well as I might have, or it could be his looks had changed. Guys like him, their looks were always changing. Or maybe I just confused one with the next, all my mother's men and those ex-cons and this one in front of me now. In my head, they were all the same man. They were all Pops. When I saw him,` the story of what happened came streaming out of me.

I'll help you, son. But you got a lesson to learn.

At his touch, I broke into a grotesque river of tears. I thought he would mock me, but no.

You're part way home, boy. Do as I say, you'll be okay. You'll make the transformation. Disappear into the walls. Into the landscape, the air and dirt. You'll be the high singing of the wires, and whatever you've lost, Christ, you'll find it again. I'll see to it. I have friends. Connections.

He could talk like that, Pops could. He could lull you to sleep with his words. The way those words washed over me, it wasn't like they came out of the darkness, but like they were the darkness, and I was sleeping inside them.

What it got down to was this. There was a young woman, and there was this movie star who wanted her dead.

It was an easy job, Pops said, it paid well, and once it was done, he would help me out of this mess.

I did what he told me. I knocked on her door. I got the wire around her neck and looked into her eyes. She reminded me of all the women I had ever known. Gloria most of all. It was her fault. If she hadn't been so sweet, I would have done it simple. I would have swindled her father and been on my way. Belle never would have discovered my past. None of this would have happened.

But it did happen. So I pulled tight, looking into her eyes. Then I put her corpse in the trunk of car and drove to the address Pops had given me.

TWENTY-SEVEN

LATE THAT AFTERNOON, Thompson made his way down a narrow side street. The Hollywood Freeway ran under an escarpment nearby, and its sound rattled the buildings. In the center of all that noise was the Satellite Bar, an ugly joint, lime green, squatting between two abandoned storefronts. Its paint was peeling, the stucco crumbling, exposing the chicken wire underneath.

Find Wicks for me, Michele Haze had told him, and I will set you free.

Inside, the Satellite Bar was empty except for the man behind the counter and the sound of the freeway. The man was as big a man as Thompson had ever seen.

"What can I do you?"

"A whiskey," Thompson said. "And a beer back."

The man stepped into the back room to get Thompson his beer, then splashed some whiskey into a glass. He wasn't exactly polite about it. He pushed the whiskey over, watched Thompson drink like a guard watches a prisoner.

"Who sent you?"

"I'm looking for Sydney Wicks."

"What's your name?"

Thompson told him.

"Who sent you?"

"She. . . I don't know if I should get into details. If you. . ."

The man cut him short. "Who sent you?"

"A client."

The guy gave him a brutish look.

"My client wants to meet with Mr. Wicks. And clear up an obligation."

"I'll make the call, but it's going to cost you a hundred bucks. She tell you that part too, this client? I don't do my work for free."

Thompson went into his envelope and counted out the money. The man stuffed the bills into his pants pocket.

"No guarantees."

The bartender stepped into a little room behind the bar. Thompson could see him through the door, hunched over the phone in a room so small it seemed barely able to contain him—and Thompson suddenly couldn't help but question the wisdom of being here. He wondered if Michele would keep her promise.

The bartender hung up and shouldered his way back towards Thompson.

"They'll call back. Meantime, you wait here."

The bartender poured himself a gin, and positioned himself at the other end of the bar, between Thompson and the door. The noise of the freeway grew louder, and a piece of stucco tumbled from an outside wall into the street. The phone rang.

"Yeah?" The bartender breathed heavily into the mouthpiece, listening. Then he hung up.

"You'll have to wait a bit longer."

"How about another round?"

The bartender splashed him a whiskey.

"And a beer to go with it?"

"I have to go to the back to get it."

"All right."

The man went into the back room. Something wasn't right. Thompson decided to leave. He stepped toward the front, but managed only a few paces before the voice boomed out.

"It's not time for you to go."

"I was just stretching."

"You can stretch sitting down."

It was a long time before the phone rang again. An eon. Three eons. The sun collapsed and was born again and every living thing turned to dust. Then it started all over, the creatures creeping up out of the big nothing, tigers with fish gills, birds with snake eyes, the whole ugly business. The jungle roared and squealed. The freeway thundered.

Finally, the call came. The conversation was as brief as before. Briefer.

"You can go now," said the bartender.

"What do you mean? What about Wicks?"

"There's no such man as Sydney Wicks. Your woman friend, she made a mistake."

Thompson decided not to argue.

TWENTY-EIGHT

THOMPSON WALKED DOWN The Strip, hands in pockets. He had to keep them there, they shook so badly. With everything that had happened, he could not help being spooked. The visit to the Satellite had changed nothing. Demons were loosed on the streets. His own demons, someone else's, it didn't matter, a little sip no longer kept things under control. The abyss was triumphant, one mean son-of-a-bitch. He tried to concentrate on events of recent days, thinking he could find in them the secret that would help him escape. No. He took out his flask. As he raised it, he saw something from the corner of his eyes. He wheeled around. Nothing. He drank. Maybe he had been wrong about everything. Though the liquid ran down his throat, following the rules of gravity, he had the opposite sensation. He felt as if his own self, his essence, were rising into the flask.

It was the same up and down the Strip. Desire turned backwards, so the thing which was desired did the consuming. He could see it in the eyes of that fat kid up ahead, lounging between the corners of Argyle and Vine. Or that woman in black leather. Or that blind man in the dead neon of the Brown Derby. Emptiness everywhere. Lounging about. Ambling. Stumbling. Eyes like broken windows. Mouths filled with the sound of Harley Davidsons. Zippers opening. A man's chest tattooed with tits big as the moon.

We're in the same boat, you and me, Thompson thought. Background characters. Nobodies. In the end we die hard deaths, exigencies of the plot.

Thompson stepped into the lobby of the Aztec Hotel. Behind the desk, the bell clerk sat upright, smoking a cigarette.

"Anybody for me?"

"No."

The kid looked pleased. His eyes glimmered, rat-like. Halfway up the stairs, Thompson turned for another look. The kid smiled. They exchanged pleasantries.

"Fuck you, kid."

"Fuck you, too, Mister."

Upstairs, Thompson found his door ajar. His room lay in shambles.

The place had been torn apart, his papers scattered, his suitcase unpacked, clothes tossed on the floor. The mattress had been pushed off the bed, the pillowcases unstuffed. The drawers hung open, the closet off its hinge.

He'd been robbed, but it didn't make sense, because he kept little of value here, and the only thing missing, so far as he could tell, was his father's Retriever. The old six-shooter was useless except as something to hang on the wall.

Thompson wondered if the bartender at the Satellite had stalled him deliberately, so someone could take apart his room. He shuffled downstairs over the worn carpet. Hands in pocket, lilting, a caterpillar walk.

"Someone ransacked my room."

"That's a shame," said the kid.

"Did you see anyone?"

"Not that I remember. But maybe I was sleeping. Or off taking a whiz. You know how it is. The help these days."

"You're a swell one, kid."

"Glad to help out."

The kid grinned malevolently, and Thompson thought maybe the boy had wrecked the room himself, to get him back for the business with the cigarette—but he could not be sure. He went back upstairs, and the telephone was ringing in his room now. He let it go a long time before picking up.

"Yeah?"

"Jim, is that you?"

Thompson recognized the voice. His agent, Matt Roach.

"Listen, I've got good news."

Thompson found it hard to believe.

"Julius Lars, over at Countdown Productions—he wants to buy *The Manifesto*. He's picking up the option. Be there tomorrow. Get yourself down to the lot. He's got some papers."

He felt a flutter in his head.

"It's been cooking for awhile. I didn't want to say anything till I was sure. I know how you've been through so many disappointments."

"What time tomorrow?"

"Ten-thirty. On the Countdown lot."

"All right."

"Meantime, courier him over the old contract, the one you signed with Miracle. There's some details to be ironed." Roach went on. Twenty grand for the story. Another fifty grand for the screenplay. Guaranteed. "You'll get it whether or not they go into production, no matter who gets the final screen credit. I put my foot down on this one."

Thompson felt his breath go out of him.

I've done it. And for a second he felt an elation so severe he all but sobbed. They could stay in the penthouse, he and Alberta. They wouldn't have to move.

He dialed Alberta and told her the news. The doubt crept over him, but he shrugged it away.

"How much?" she asked.

"Seventy thousand."

"That's a lot of money."

"Cancel the movers."

"It's too late. They're coming tomorrow. And I've already given notice to the landlord."

"Stall him."

"I can't."

"Yes, you can. Don't you see, honey? We've got it made."

"All right."

"I want you to go with me to the studio."

"You don't want me there, not while you're signing the papers."

"The Countdown lot is clear the other side of town."

It took some talking, but she agreed; she would pick him up in the morning. As soon as he was off the phone, though, he thought of the Mexican border, and Lussie Jones.

Her husband would be in town now. Tomorrow evening there was that dance, in the old Crystal Ballroom, not far from the Château. I'll go, Thompson thought.

I'll cut in. I'll steal her away.

He looked down. His papers lay scattered all over the floor, and his doubt returned. He gathered the manuscript up. In these pages, his book imitated the scene at the Hillcrest Arms. There was confusion at the pay-off point. Pops vanished, the corpse too. The killer wandered the city, looking for his money. Life and fiction overlapped. The events in *The Manifesto,* and the events of the last few days were converging. Who was Wicks? And where had he gone? Thompson went into the closet. In the far back, wedged into a dark corner, he found a paper sack his visitor had missed. Soon as he felt the bag, he remembered. The dead girl's sweater. He had taken it from the Cadillac, then misplaced it in his room.

He pulled it out of the bag. It was an expensive

sweater, otherwise unremarkable, except for one thing he hadn't noticed up on the hill: a single initial embroidered across the breast.

C.

The Young Lovely, what was her real name? Anna, or Amanda, or Annabelle—something like that, he couldn't be sure.

And her last name?

Thompson didn't know. He paced the room. Maybe I am wrong about the initials, he thought, and wrong about other things as well, and he wondered if he should call Michele Haze and tell her what had happened at the Satellite. He wondered too if the Cadillac had been discovered.

Then he lay back and told himself none of that mattered. He had hit the big time. People in the big time, guys like me, they always escape in the end. Then he told himself the same thing again, one more time, just to be sure.

TWENTY-NINE

THE NEXT MORNING, ALBERTA picked him up in Mrs. Myers' sedan. She drove with a skeptical demeanor, her hands high on the wheel, gripping tightly, like a woman taking a jalopy through a town she had not seen before, and did not much like. She wore a polka dot dress and a string of pearls. Her face had a hard beauty.

"Is this on the level?"

"Matt says so."

"He's been wrong before."

"I know."

"I'm just wondering."

"We struck a gusher, honey. It's that simple."

Alberta yanked the sedan up to the curb.

"I'll wait here."

"Come inside with me."

"This is your moment."

"I want you with me. At least wait in the office."

"No."

Thompson climbed out. A restaurant stood at the corner, a half-block away, and his eyes caught movement in the window, or maybe it was the premonition of movement, and he had the feeling you get at crowded terminals sometimes, far from home, as if maybe you will cross paths with someone you know, here in this unexpected place. The street stood empty.

Thompson went through the studio gate. Julius Lars had his office at the far end of the lot, but it was nothing special, just a trailer up on blocks. That was the way Countdown ran things. He found Julius at the rear of the trailer with his shirt sleeves rolled up, in front of a Formica desk. They had met before.

"Good to see you, Julius."

"You too, Jim."

Julius wore a white shirt open at the collar. He was a friendly enough guy usually, with a broad smile and a bulbous nose, but his expression at the moment was grim. He had a wild shock of hair, and he ran his fingers through it now as if all that hair belonged to someone else.

"Your agent talk to you?"

"Yeah."

"This morning?"

"Last night. What's up?"

"The paperwork."

"Well, I'm sure we can work it out."

"I don't know."

Julius slid the paper across the desk. It was the contract Thompson had signed for Miracle that day in Musso's, the offending parts highlighted now in yellow.

"You signed the rights away."

"What?"

"The story doesn't belong to you."

"But Lombard canceled the deal. He never signed with Miracle."

"It doesn't matter. Your deal—it's with Miracle."

"Jesus."

"I'm sorry, Jim."

Julius put his hand on Thompson's shoulder. "Maybe we can work on another project together, later. This one, if we were to do it, would have to go through Billy." Julius kept talking, but Thompson wasn't listening anymore. The man guided him through the trailer, into the lot. Future possibilities, he said. This project. That. Together, you and me. Thompson smiled, nodded. Something shifted inside him. Ten steps, twelve. He found himself outside the studio gate, alone, dizzy. His gut hurt bad, as if the air'd been punched out. Alberta glanced his way. Flowing out of the car in her polka dot dress. Guessing how it was with him, figuring the whole business. He loped towards her, bent over at the shoulder, swinging one arm—and he felt something lurch within him now. A stroke, he feared, his arm going numb. Then, lifting his head, squinting, he caught a man emerging from the cafe. Running down the sidewalk. A flash of metal.

Thompson had known about the contract, or he should have known, if he'd bothered to think it through, just as he'd known that sooner or later this man would find him on the street. How he had come to be here, whether by design or coincidence, Thompson didn't know. It didn't matter. The street was no longer empty. The Okie brushed past Alberta, grabbed Thompson by the collar.

"It's you, old man. I saw you from the restaurant window. 'Howdy-doody.' I said to myself. Son of a bitch." The Okie shook with a horrible excitement, then pressed a gun into Thompson's gut. "Where's my car? Who you working for?"

It no longer mattered if the history he'd invented for this man were real or imagined. The Okie looked at him hard, then the man's eyes went soft and watery, other-worldly, just as they had done back at the Hillcrest apartment, before the cops sent him running. The dead girl had seen this look too, no doubt, the swimming in the eyes, in the instant before he strangled her. Alberta called out. The Okie turned his head, shifted his balance, and Alberta came around with her purse. Thompson fell, hitting the ground, rolling to his side, clutching his gut, hearing Alberta yell out as if from a great distance, "Jim! Jim!" but he was plummeting through the darkness once more, forever, it seemed, past the sound of receding footsteps, soles slapping on the pavement, to a depth where there were no more sounds, no words, nothing left to say.

THIRTY

THOMPSON WOKE UP in the emergency ward, underground, in the cellar of the Hollywood Presbyterian Hospital. Alberta sat in a metal chair nearby, not looking at Thompson, though, but at the ruddy-faced resident, all in white, who sat in the chair beside her.

"I managed to get in touch with Doctor Rufus, your husband's regular physician. He tells me there's a history of alcoholism?"

"Yes," said Alberta. "But I don't know if this is related. You see, like I said, a man attacked us on the street. He had a gun. I knocked it loose. He gathered it up, and ran."

"I understand. The good news, though, is that there are no signs of injury. No external trauma."

"Did he have a stroke?"

"I've seen it happen. An older person gets mugged, their house burns down, something like that, it triggers a stroke. But my feeling, what we have here is nervous exhaustion. Complicated by the alcoholism. Doctor Rufus suspects other underlying problems as well. Ulcerated stomach. Pulmonary deterioration—and these may be related to the collapse."

"I see."

"Dr. Rufus thinks it may be time to get your husband into a treatment center. He suggests Mr. Thompson stay overnight for observation. In the morning, we'll do a thorough check-up. If he's strong enough—if there isn't an immediate medical problem—then your husband should go to a sanitarium."

Thompson didn't like the idea. He tried to speak. The resident hovered over him, a blur of white, and Thompson got a glimpse of the man's hand reaching out to adjust the i-v. The resident was still talking, and Alberta said something in response, but their voices sounded far away now, then farther, as if they were talking outside the door, down the hall, the next county over, and pretty soon he no longer heard them at all.

•

He awoke later in another room, higher up in the building, the curtains drawn, the light around their edges bright and important. Mid-afternoon. Alberta and the resident gone, i-v disconnected. A chair empty by the closed door.

He slept.

The sun crept around the other side of the building. The room went gray and murky. He woke again and stared up into that murk for a long time, then turned his head to the door.

Lieutenant Orville Mann sat in the chair. The atmosphere of the room, the state of his own mind, were both such that Thompson assumed Mann was not actually there. I am dreaming, he thought, moving from one state of consciousness to another.

"They told me I could have a few minutes."

Thompson touched himself. The way the resident had been talking earlier, he worried he had gone over the edge, into delirium. He'd seen the Okie, though, he was sure of that. Mann, he decided now, was real.

"What happened out on the sidewalk?"

"I don't know."

"You have enemies? You know the man who attacked you?"

"No," Thompson lied.

"We had your wife look through some mug shots.

There's a half dozen strong-arm artists work the streets down in that area."

"She recognize anyone?"

"No. But we put a description in the neighborhood. Got one call. A lady said she saw someone like your man hitchhiking on the Hollywood on-ramp. Headed north."

"You think it was him?"

"Can't say. My guess, whoever it was, he'll show up in Bakersfield, some damn place. Probably pull the same stunt all over again." Mann fingered his hat as he spoke. "You know, that's quite a woman you've got there."

"Uh-hum."

"Salt of the earth." The cop was at it again, trying to wear him down, one homily at a time.

"She's my better half, all right,"

"The wisdom of the world is in a woman's nod."

"That's true. You've hit it on the head."

"Uh-huh."

"A woman like that," said Thompson, "she keeps the lead in your pencil."

The Lieutenant bowed his head. His eyes grew solemn, like a rube who'd glimpsed a woman's petticoats—and he put the routine away. "They had a memorial service for Jack Lombard today. Half the town was there, including Lombard's girlfriends. Both of them."

"Both?"

"Yes, Michele Haze. And Anita Smith. They kissed and hugged." The cop shook his head, bemused. "Only in Hollywood."

Anita Smith. Thompson grabbed at the name. People in the business, they seldom called the woman by her real name, but that's who she was. The Young Lovely wasn't dead after all; that's why the initials didn't match.

But who was the woman in the Cadillac?

"It seems Miss Smith left Hollywood a few days before Lombard's murder. I'm not telling you anything new here, it's in the gossip sheets all over town these last few days. I guess they had some kind of lover's spat."

"I wasn't aware."

"They made up on the phone, long distance. They were going to get married, soon as she got back. Poor girl—but that's not the end of it. She gets back here, to her place in Topanga Canyon, and it turns out her roommate has disappeared too."

"Roommate?"

"Another girl, looking for a break in Hollywood. You know how it is, one leaves, another takes her place. This one, though, she didn't stick around long."

"What do you mean?"

"Vanished," Lieutenant Man shrugged. "Miss Smith says that's not surprising. She's that kind. Four addresses in the last year and a half. She blows in, she blows out."

Thompson closed his eyes. It occurred to him now: the Okie had killed the wrong woman.

"Cathy," said Lieutenant Mann. "Cathy Hanfield. That's the missing woman. You know her?"

"No."

He was a fuck-up, the Okie. The loose nut, the wild card, dust in the clockwork. He'd been hired to kill The Young Lovely, but he'd gotten her roommate instead. Delivered her to the wrong address.

"You're looking a little pale."

"I've had a hard day."

"I just have a few more questions. You know, they told me, when you checked into the hospital—you had all your identification loose in your pocket. You weren't carrying a wallet?"

"No."
"Why not?'
"My old one fell apart." Thompson reached for the call button; he wanted to get rid of the cop.
"We found some prints on the murder weapon. We sent them over to the federal print lab, looking for a match." Lieutenant Mann smiled his country boy smile. "And something else. We found a shoe. A man's shoe. In the bushes."
"That right?"
"Yeah. Seems it belonged to a big man. Someone with good size feet."
Thompson squirmed. My feet, he thought. Big as Jesus, right here, hidden beneath the bed sheets.
Where was the goddamn nurse?
"You know, it's a shame the way they treat you. These Hollywood people hold out promises, then they pull the string. You ever been fingerprinted?"
"No."
"You wouldn't mind if I do that now, for our records?"
It would be best to co-operate, Thompson figured, but he wasn't sure what had happened that night in Beverly Hills. For all he knew, Miracle had placed the weapon in his hands while he lay unconscious, transferring the prints.
Thompson didn't know what to do. His moves were getting fewer, the trap tighter. Then the nurse walked in, a grim redhead—but pretty in her own gloomy way. "Visiting hours are over. Two hours ago."
"Guilty," Lieutenant Mann raised his hands in a gesture of surrender. "I admit it. I overstayed my time."
"You snuck by the desk?" she demanded.
"I don't deny it. You know how they say," he glanced toward Thompson, "if the shoe fits. . ."

"Go," the nurse said. She turned to Thompson. "You pressed the call button?"

"I was just wondering how long before supper."

"I'll be bringing it in a few minutes. Along with your evening medication."

Thompson didn't want to stay here overnight. He hadn't had a drink since this morning, and by tomorrow, first light, withdrawal would be on him; he would be clutterheaded, clamoring at the walls. No, he couldn't go to the sanitarium, not now. Besides, a line of reasoning had begun to form in his head, an avenue of escape.

He had to go back up the hill, to Whitley Terrace.

His stomach churned at the idea, he needed to think it through more clearly, but now the nurse returned with his tray. Alongside his soup, a paper medicine cup. Inside the cup, two yellow pills.

"I'll need for you to take this medication."

"What is it?"

"Something to help you sleep."

Thompson did not resist. He put the pills to his mouth and swallowed and afterwards took a big drink of water. The redhead watched, hands on hips, prettier than before but also more grim, eyes gray and empty-hearted as an Iowa sky. There was no cheering her up, but it did not matter. He remembered the routine from his last time around at the sanitarium, when the attendant had come around with his nightly dose of anabuse. Just like then, when the nurse left, Thompson opened his hand.

The yellow pills lay still in his palm.

THIRTY-ONE

SOMETIME AFTER MIDNIGHT, Thompson changed into his street clothes. He waited till the night nurse was on her break, then he sneaked past her desk, down the antiseptic corridors. He saw now why the redhead was so gloomy. They had lodged her—and himself, too—on the floor of hopeless cases. Old ladies with rosary beads, kids without legs. People crushed by coincidence, by the falling moon. A couple of orderlies lazed about in the lobby, but they gave him only the barest of glances. Outside, he grabbed a bus back to Hollywood. Something like pain tickled his gut, also the craving for a drink, but neither sensation was as strong as it might be. The hospital dope, all that stuff they'd pumped into him all day long, to ease him into withdrawal, it was doing its business—but he knew it would wear off before long. He would need the yellow pills.

At the Aztec, he retrieved the cashmere sweater. He hunted out a pocket flashlight at the corner market, also a brand new pint. Halfway up Grace Avenue, he stopped to catch his breath. The lights of the city lurched in the darkness below. His hands shook. He had no taste for what lay ahead. According to Lieutenant Mann, the Okie had left town, and The Young Lovely was still alive. Both these things were to his advantage. Because if The Young Lovely was not dead, Michele Haze could not be implicated in her murder. She was free to tell the police what had really happened that night at Lombard's.

There was one complication, though. The girl in the Cadillac. If her body were discovered, the whole thing might come unraveled.

Thompson uncorked the flask. The hill crested, and he swiveled along the gravel road, into the dark.

He had to bury the girl.

There were no houses along here, no moon. The eucalyptus grew thickly along the road, blotting out the stars. He came upon the Cadillac suddenly, hulking up out of the darkness, and all but speared himself on the tail fin. He felt along its side until he reached the door. The keys hung in the ignition, just as he had left them.

He went around to the back and popped the trunk. The smell was overpowering, and he retched in the high grass.

He had not used the flashlight earlier, fearing it might call attention. Now he ran the narrow beam over her body, looking for that shovel he had seen that first day. He wriggled it loose and headed down the hill to find the open trench. He lay the shovel down. Went back for the girl.

It was not easy work. Her body was bloated, the skin moist. He reached into the trunk and struggled her free. She had been wearing a skirt when she died, and he gripped her thighs to his chest as he stumbled away from the Cadillac. The smell overcame him again. He lay her down, and went back to the weeds. Then splashed whiskey onto his face, around his nostrils. Wrapped her in the sheet the murderer had left behind, covering her face, her skin, hefting her up now, fireman style, at the same time clutching the flashlight in one hand, the light bobbing wildly as he jerked and stumbled down the path.

He was a big man, she a little woman. If not for that, he might never have managed. He hobbled along the ridge towards the open trench the highway workers had left behind, her arms and legs working their way out of the sheet, swinging stiff. His heart hammered, the blood rushed to his head. *You got yourself a stroke in the making*, the doctor had told him. Thompson felt its inevitability. He would collapse. Spend the rest of his days unable to pick up a pencil, stare out at the street from his window at the Hillcrest Arms. Perhaps he lay already in that sick bed, this moment struggling up the hill, all these moments, were not real but imagined, images glimpsed from beneath fluttering eyelids, forgotten the second he opened his eyes.

He reached the trench. He went shakily to his knees, lowering his burden. The sheet fell away and she lay in front of him now, arms spread wide, hair in a bouffant, lipstick feathered sloppily about her lips. Her face was swollen and puffy. Her corpse wore the expression of one who had just learned a secret so hideous and awful she yearned to whisper it over and over and never stop. He pushed her into the trench. She tumbled in, down in to the blackness. She landed face up. He threw the embroidered sweater after her and began to cover her with dirt.

It wasn't just the girl he was burying, he told himself, it was the whole shebang. Miracle and the Okie. Michele Haze. Alberta. Mom and Dad and the state of Oklahoma. All those black pages, three million words. A dream he'd had once upon a time on a hillside, wrapping its legs around him in the velvet night.

Shovel after shovel. Dirt in his nose and the smell of exhaust rising in the canyon. Arduous work for an old man, but he accomplished it somehow. He buried the girl.

Thompson climbed up the hill to the Cadillac. He smoked a cigarette and crushed it in the dirt. He took a drink, then suddenly he was overcome once more.

He retched again.

The girl was an innocent. She had her flaws, no doubt. A big nose, maybe, unrealistic dreams. She'd wanted a role in Hollywood. A moment at the center of things. Well, she'd gotten her wish, more or less.

He started the car and drove down to Watts, to where the riots had raged a few years back. The area was still gutted. The buildings lay in ruins. He kept all the windows open, hoping to get rid of the smell, but it seemed to be in the air itself now. He parked the Caddy on Bleaker Street, not far from the Watts Towers. Then he dropped the keys into a grate and flagged down a taxi.

The Cadillac would be stripped. It would disappear piece by piece. Tires and hubcaps, carburetor, hood ornaments and all. Within days, it would look like the other cars that lined the streets, here in this neighborhood of abandoned cars. Sooner or later, the police would come out to get it, and maybe someone would tell them they'd seen a white man drop it off, but it wouldn't matter. They'd drag it down to impound, run a trace on the serial. Maybe they'd find the owner, maybe they wouldn't, but either way it would all be settled by the insurance company. Routine case, stolen car, junked and abandoned in Watts. That would be the end of it, or close enough, because they would never trace the car to Michele Haze, or to himself. Because the girl was a nobody. No one was looking for her, not even the cops.

Thompson went back to the Aztec Hotel. The hospital should've discovered his absence by now. They would call Alberta, and she would track him here. So he gathered up his typewriter and checked himself a room in the flophouse across the street. He swallowed the sleeping tablets he had palmed at the hospital.

Then he remembered Lussie. It was the night of the dance. He would never see her now. He had known it all along. She would spin around that dance floor without him, fly back to Lincoln.

Lucille Jones. He'd had his chance in New York. The reason he had not taken it was because it was no chance at all. The girl she'd been was dead, and that woman, leaning against the wall, eyes shimmering, knew it as well as he did. Because there had been something else in her eyes that he had not admitted until now.

If he had tried, Lussie would have pushed him away. Same as she had years before. Still, she had been disappointed, he guessed, by the slouch of her evening gown, the jangle of her pearls.

Anyway it was done. He had other things to tend to now. He would call Alberta. He would check into the sanitarium, he told himself, quit drinking, avoid that stroke that lay ahead. First, though, there were loose ends. He had to see Michele Haze. He called her service, left a message. Then he fell into a deep and tumultuous sleep, in which he was an old man, struggling with a corpse of a young woman, dragging her along a hillside, dragging her over and over again. She was beautiful, almost, and she spoke to him, whispering in the language of the gullies, of the weed grass and the oil cans.

I forgive you. But he knew it was not true. Her arms had him about the neck, and she would never let him go.

THIRTY-TWO

I ended up on the highway again, where it all started, thumb out. A man picked me up this time, a salesman. Starched white shirt. Yellow tie. Hair slicked back, cowlick sticking straight up.

Insurance, he said, that was his game. He liked to see people well protected. And he liked to talk.

"Name's Hank. Hank Goodfellow. Where you headed?"

I didn't answer, but Mr. Goodfellow didn't seem to care. He just kept talking. Himself, he was headed out to Phoenix, he said, because there were lots of retired folks out that way who appreciated the value of a good annuity.

"Peace of mind, that's what people want in their Golden Years. Serenity. Except some of these elder types, they'll pull your tail. Ace the company right out of its dough, you know what I mean."

We kept driving, and he kept talking, and the meanwhile I wondered if that's what Pops was doing, living it up on the money I was supposed to have been paid for taking care of that girl.

I hadn't heard from him, not a word, not even his voice inside my head.

The silence was getting to me.

"The only disadvantage to this traveling life," said Hank Goodfellow, "is a man gets lonely. He misses his wife and kids."

Mr. Goodfellow reached down towards his ass and tugged at his wallet.

"What you doin'?"

"Photos," he grinned, and out they came. The family all dressed up, sitting in front of some photographer's backdrop at the local department store.

"Come on. Those ain't your wife and kids."

"Yes, they are."

"No, they ain't."

He stuck his lip out, offended. Wondering to himself just why he'd picked up a guy like me.

Myself, I was thinking about that business on the street, before I left L.A. I'd seen the old man before, I thought, back at the apartment, where I'd taken that girl's corpse, and I was pretty sure he was hooked into the routine. He was hooked up with Pops somehow, or maybe he even was Pops. Then I'd looked into those watery eyes and seen the confusion there, and realized he was nobody, just some old fool. And something else occurred to me. Maybe old Pops was everywhere, little bits and pieces of him, chopped up and living inside each of us. I grabbed the old man, trying to shake the truth out of him, but then the old woman came out of nowhere, worthless hag, and knocked me upside the head with her purse.

So now here I was, on the road again. Goodfellow driving fast, hauling bloody murder through the desert, the hot wind whipping through the windows. I looked him over more carefully. My height, my weight. Except for his clothes, he was a kind of mirror of myself. There was a difference though. He was a real, solid guy, with responsibilities, a job to do, a regular position. Me, I was just some figment, a shadow passing through his life.

The idea infuriated me, and I yanked out my gun.

We turned off into that desert then, and as we moved further from the main highway, I imagined all the creatures crawling across the hot sand, and I thought I could hear the sounds they made, the slithering and hissing. I was like them, I told myself. I needed to survive. Food. Shelter. But it wasn't just those things.

I needed some kind of explanation. A reason for the way things were.

"Right here." I directed Goodfellow down a dirt road. About a half mile in, the road started to peter away.

"You ever hear a voice in your head? Tells you what to do, how to live your life? You fight it, you resist, finally hell, one day, you just give in. 'Okay,' you say. 'Stop pestering me. I'll listen, I'll do anything you like.' So you do that, you make the big leap, then the son of a bitch abandons you. You ever have an experience like that?"

He nodded obligingly. There was sweat on his brow.

"You ain't just saying that, are you?"

He shook his head.

"Good. Because I want to hear that voice again, you and me. Where better to listen, then here, in the middle of all this quiet. Now, pull over. Get out and take off your clothes."

"Please, no."

"I like yours better than mine. We're gonna trade."

"I got a wife. A child."

"No you don't."

He did what I told him, took off his clothes and stood stark naked under the desert sun. Then we put on each other's clothes, and traded wallets, too. He had an expectant look in his eyes, as if part of him were waiting for something to happen. Like maybe something would swoop down from the sky and chariot him away. Except no one came, of course, and I let him stand there until I could see in his eyes he was thinking things over more realistically. Maybe the most realistic thoughts he'd ever had in his life.

"Come on," I said. "Tell me what you hear."

He whimpered.

"What's it saying? Come on, now."

Hank Goodfellow stood there in the heat, his eyes earnest, his face pale. His lips parted, trembling, like maybe he had something he wanted to say. Like maybe he had heard the voice and was ready to tell me what he'd heard. Then he shrugged his shoulders and bolted for the ravine.

I fired. He kept running, but he was staggering, and I fired again. This time he fell down. He got up again, scrambling on all fours, but he was gut shot. He tumbled into the ravine and I found him there at the bottom on his back, grunting. The blood frothed up out of his mouth. He started to choke and gasp, wheeze and strangle, making all kinds of ungodly sounds, but I sat there listening, patiently, until he was quiet and his eyes began to glaze.

I had heard something, I thought, there in the empty spaces, in the silence between each gasp and rattle, and I heard it now too, in the desert air, in the hot sand, where the creatures hissed and vanished.

Then, it was gone. No voice at all, really, just the promise of a voice.

I cursed for a little while, pissed off. I fell to my knees and sobbed, but my sobbing died away, and I felt the hot wind on my cheeks, the faintest whisper, my sobs echoing back, and I knew I couldn't give up.

I would have to go on looking, listening. There were more streets for me to wander, I knew, doors to unlock, windows to crawl through. On the other sides of those windows and doors, more people, men and women who had the truth inside them, maybe, but didn't want to admit it, or wouldn't know it until they heard it from their own lips. So I had to get them to talk. It was a job without end.

Meanwhile, I had my new clothes, my new wallet. A position in the world. I climbed into the car. Then I started up the engine and drove off into all that mindless dust.

The next afternoon, Thompson slid the final pages into the mail slot, his obligation fulfilled. His mind quavered. The killer had been a miserable sort from the opening pages—or maybe the world had conspired against him, one bad break after another—but either way, he had graduated to the next level, so to speak. A man on a mission, loose in the world. Himself, Thompson, he was worn out. His evening on the hill had left him sore and dirty. It had gone as well as such a thing could go, he supposed. Even so, he felt undone. The air tremored with an unnatural clarity, and the light shimmered, as if the walls themselves were on the verge of speaking. He took a drink. The shadows hissed.

Alberta was right. *The Manifesto* would not save them from the Hillcrest Arms. Still, he had kept up his end. Miracle owed him a grand. If the producer didn't pay—couldn't, or wouldn't, no matter—then the book would be Thompson's. He could shop it all he pleased.

He dialed Michele Haze.

"Just a minute, Mr. Thompson."

Her answering service again. The line went quiet. A shadow moved. He heard other voices, on the phone, in the background, maybe, here in the room. He couldn't tell. The receptionist returned. "Yes, Michele Haze wants very much to meet with you."

"When?"

"Three-thirty this afternoon. At her business suite in Santa Monica. The Alameda Building. You know it?"

"Yes."

"Room 47."

She rang off. He listened to the room. There'd been no other voices after all, he decided. Just cars whispering down the street, curtains rustling. He had the shakes pretty bad. Maybe it had been his own bones he'd heard, rattling away. He sipped. Careful not to drink too much, just enough. Ease the rattling. Becalm the light. He needed to talk to Michele, explain the situation. You can talk to the cops now, honey, he would tell her; you're off the hook. Then he could forget it all. Let the demons run. Meantime, he took another sip. To steady himself. To keep the light and the dark separated, the voices quiet.

THIRTY-THREE

THE ALAMEDA WAS AN IMPROBABLE looking building in the style known as California Gothic, squat and wide, with elephantine columns and a red tile roof. A trellis, made of wood and strap leather, slouched morosely over the entry. Thompson recognized the building's ugliness, but appreciated its stolidity. His shakes had left him, but the light falling through the flowering yuccas was wild and bright.

The Alameda was not Michele's main residence. That would be in the hills somewhere. This was an apartment suite she kept for doing business.

He stepped under the trellis. The security system was nothing elaborate, just a buzzer and a squawk box.

Thompson rang. The door opened.

Inside, he pigeon-toed his way through the lobby into an open-air courtyard. It was more splendid than he expected: palm trees and staircases spiraling toward iron balconies hung with jasmine and trumpet vine. The layout, though, was confusing, and he could not figure how to proceed. Each suite opened to its own balcony, and each balcony had its own gate, with steps descending to the central staircase, which in turn descended to the courtyard. Trouble was, the gates were not numbered. Thompson had no idea which one belonged to Michele Haze.

He retreated to the lobby, and a creaking elevator. It carried him up to the fourth floor, where the door to Michele's suite stood ajar.

"Anyone home?"

In the entry were pictures of Michele Haze from earlier in her career. Eyes like the eyes he had seen in the limousine, glancing over her shoulder through the blue neon.

Thompson heard something. Feet shuffling. Shoes on carpet.

A narrow hall led away from the parlor. It opened onto the dining room. When Thompson turned the corner, the first thing he saw was himself—in a mirror that gaped across the opposite wall, floor to ceiling. At the far end of the table, a chair had been overturned, but that was not what drew his attention. Rather it was Michele Haze, lying stiff-legged on the carpet, one hand underneath her stomach. She lay in a pool of red. Her hair was bloody, and her clothes, too, and there was blood seeping into the carpet.

Thompson saw movement in the mirror. A man stepping out of the shadows, into the reflection.

Billy Miracle.

He held a revolver in his hand. "Nice gun," Miracle said. "Family heirloom, is it?"

Thompson felt an odd calm. The gun Miracle held, it was a Retriever. Alberta had mentioned it at Musso's. The hotel clerk was the one who'd ransacked his apartment, he had thought, or the Okie—but he'd been wrong. It was Miracle.

"It's little rusty-looking, this old pistol," the producer said. "But it works swell."

Miracle twitched, blinked. His eyes, moist and black, shone with a certain irreality—a preternatural alertness. Thompson followed his gaze as it skittered over the dead woman. Her posture was long and thin. She wore a beige skirt and a blouse the same color, with a hint of pink. Her blonde hair spewed on to the carpet. Her face was turned from Thompson, but he could see it in the mirror—just as he could see Miracle standing behind him. The star's face bore a look of anguish. Her eyes were still open, her hands clenched, one in a fist beneath her stomach, the other grabbing at the hem of her skirt, as if she'd been twisting it in her fingers as she died. The skirt lay hiked now well above the knee.

Miracle had shot her. She had grabbed the chair for support, maybe, but it had toppled, then she had fallen to the floor. She'd been dead, or dying, Thompson thought, when I rang the door.

My bad luck to stumble into the middle of their argument. An instant's contemplation, though, told him it had nothing to do with luck. Miracle had used Thompson's gun, after all. He'd buzzed him in, as if he expected his arrival. So Miracle had planned it, just as he'd planned the other deaths, one scheme after another, begun in simple desperation—his need to make the film, to satisfy his mobster partner—but ending here, in this labyrinth in which Thompson found himself now. Miracle stood between Thompson and the front door. He wondered if there were another way out. He remembered the balconies, the interconnecting staircases.

"You killed her," said Miracle. The producer dressed as always. White jacket, black shirt. Gold necklace and cream-colored slacks. "You came in here, and you murdered the poor girl."

"No."

Behind him, he could feel Miracle's physical presence—while at the same time the man's image loomed in the mirror before him. Another mirror hung on the far wall behind them both. Their images repeated inside it, receding in infinite regression.

"So far as I can tell, it started with that killer," Miracle said. "The one you hired to take care of The Young Lovely. That's how the police will see it, I'm sure. You and Michele, you arranged it together."

"That's not what happened." Thompson protested. Miracle did not seem to hear. His chest swelled grandly.

"Each of you had your own reasons. Michele—she wanted rid of the girl. She wanted her man back, her position on the throne. You, on the other hand—-a desperate writer, at the end of his string. The Young Lovely was blocking your path. And if you got rid of her, well, not only would she be gone, but Michele would be indebted to you too. But you didn't anticipate what would happen next. That Michele would get back with Jack, then cut you out of the picture altogether. Cancel the deal. So you went into a rage. A bloody, alcoholic rage. You went up to Lombard's house, and you killed the son of a bitch. And when it was all done, you collapsed in the front yard. You left your wallet behind, your shoes. You made a bloody fucking mess of the business."

It hadn't happened that way. Miracle was reversing the roles, making Thompson out to be the guilty party. "You're trying to frame me," Thompson's voice cracked, his hands trembled, but he still felt calm. He observed his shaking hands as if they belonged to someone else. "You're the one, Billy."

Miracle ignored him. "Then the police began to close in, and you became more desperate. Your trump card was Michele. Or so you thought. She would defend you. She would provide you with an alibi the night of Lombard's murder. Because after all, she had helped plan the death of The Young Lovely—and if she turned against you now, well, you'd tell the police. But then, that too went astray. Because it turns out your killer—the klutz, the bumbler, the fool—he killed the wrong woman. Some passerby, a woman no one knows, no one cares about. Even her body has disappeared—and how could you threaten Michele with complicity in a murder that never happened? So you begged her to help. You pleaded, but you began to suspect she was going to let you fall. Then—you killed her. You shot her with your father's gun."

Miracle's version of events had its own inner logic. A flawed logic, sure, but it was the logic that controlled the moment. He could feel its inexorable movement forward. Whether the police would realize this or not, he had no idea, because he knew (and the cops knew) such falterings in logic underlie not just the ravings of lunatics, but the case of the most assiduous prosecutor. There was in every argument a place between the seams, where the clutter lay. No matter how you tried to fill it up with detail, to bridge the abyss, to cover the gap, it was still there.

Himself, he had always been drawn to that place, to that little crack in the fabric of things, the inevitable flaw in the glass.

"You think you know what the dead are asking for?" Miracle asked.

Thompson shook his head. Miracle had gone off the edge. His own knees were knocking now, and he felt a trembling in his chest. His calm had dissipated.

"It isn't justice the dead want. It isn't some kind of explanation. No—it's much simpler than that. The dead, they're tired of being dead. They want to come back."

Thompson looked at the gun in the man's hand.

"But the dead can't come back, so they want the next best thing. They want company, my friend—they want someone to pay them a visit. So they send their emissaries, spokesmen on their behalf. Cancer. Strokes. Epilepsy. The bogey man in the closet with a long knife. We pretend to ourselves we don't recognize their voices, but we do. The force of all the souls calling out, it's irresistible. Their numbers get bigger all the time, the chorus deafening. There's no choice but to join them.

"A guy like you, you understand what I'm saying, don't you Jimbo."

Meanwhile, the grimace on Michele's face seemed to have grown tighter, more grotesque. There was blood clotting in her hair, between her teeth. She had gotten it all over herself, rolling about, dying on the carpet.

"It's the women who provide our inspiration, don't they? But in the end, we have to take the trip back ourselves. Make the big plunge."

"Why don't you put down the gun?"

"You aren't going soft on me, are you? Don't tell me, underneath it all, you're a sap, too. You want to ride into that beautiful sunset. Talk to God. Get a place in Malibu."

"I think we should call the police."

"We will. Or I will. Do you want to know what I'm going to tell them, about today?"

Thompson nodded, just to delay the man. He saw his head move in the mirror, and in the mirror opposite, the images embedded one inside the other, all those images of himself moving in unison, and he wondered what it was he had thought himself aspiring to, really, all those days at Musso's. He wondered if there was some golden world, just beyond his reach—or if instead it was just the same world, refracting back onto itself over and over, and the deeper into it you wandered, the more entrapped you became, until finally, one day, the corpse you stumbled over was your own, and you found yourself on the floor, staring into your own face, your own eyes, and in those eyes were the retreating feet of Billy Miracle.

"You see, Michele and I, we have the same answering service. I'm friendly with the girl who picks up the phone. When I called this morning, the receptionist told me you and Michele were having a meeting. It worried me, you've been so erratic lately, so odd and temperamental. So I hurried over.

"Unfortunately, I got here a little bit late. Or that's what I'll tell the cops. Michele was dead, and you were standing there with your gun. I tried to talk you into turning yourself in, but you wouldn't listen. We tussled. The gun went off. Down you fell. Right there, right next to Michele."

The flaw in his logic was still there, underneath all that detail, and Thompson knew now how Miracle meant to keep it from becoming visible.

He was going to kill Jim Thompson.

It was like something out of one of his own books, the killer pulling a double murder, then rearranging the corpses so it looked like one had killed the other. Truth was, such schemes rarely worked. There was always hell to pay: men who analyzed the angle of fallen bodies, the splatter of blood, the residue of gunpowder upon the hand. None of that made any difference now, though, in the land of the mirror, where Miracle spun his story and Thompson stood listening.

Thompson remembered something else. Miracle had called him at home, back when this whole thing had started. Alberta had given him the address of the Hillcrest Arms. That meeting had never materialized, but it was the last piece of the puzzle. Because when Alberta told him the address, Miracle must have written it down. On the backside of the same paper where he had written the address of the El Rancho Motel. Where the corpse was to be delivered.

"You're Sydney Wicks," Thompson said.

Miracle's eyes glinted, and he knew it was true. Miracle had used the name of Sydney Wicks when he set up the murder. He'd given the delivery address to his contact at the Satellite, and the contact had given it to the Okie, not realizing Thompson's address had been scrawled on the other side. Then the Okie had flipped the paper over, and driven to the wrong place.

"Turn around," said Billy Miracle.

Thompson hesitated. The whole conversation so far had taken place in the mirror. He feared what would happen when he faced the man directly.

"At the Satellite, it was you the man called. And you ransacked my room. Stole my gun."

"Turn around. Or I'll plug you in the back."

Thompson obeyed. He did not know what else to do. The tremor was on the surface now. He shivered hard, and shivered some more, and his body felt no longer his own. The walls vibrated, the room swooned, and every shadow had something to say.

"I need a drink," said Thompson.

"Not now. There's no time."

Miracle approached him, swaying as he walked. Thompson stepped away. "It won't work. No one will believe you."

Thompson moved towards the hall, but Miracle moved with him. There was nowhere to go. Miracle stood at point blank range. If he takes another step forward, Thompson thought, maybe I can reach out, knock the gun away. Miracle lunged. Thompson backed up instinctively, his hands rising at his sides, and there was an instant in which Miracle glanced at him, his eyes moist, his lips parted, when Thompson thought it impossible the other man would shoot. No. It couldn't happen.

Miracle fired.

Thompson felt the recoil in his chest, and heard the explosion loud in his head, and saw the astonished look on the producer's face. Staggering, glancing towards the far mirror, he saw too his own gruesome expression. The room filled with noise. I'll die looking in the mirror. Me too, just like Michele. He expected to see blood blossoming on his chest. But no, there was no blood. The noise came from Miracle. Howling, reeling away, holding the gun in his hand, a blister of flesh. His father's gun had misfired.

He might have escaped out the front door, but Miracle lurched clumsily towards the hall, blocking Thompson's path. The producer fell to his knees in pain. Thompson ran to the other end of the flat, looking for the balcony. He yanked open the living room drapes, but they revealed only a picture window overlooking the street. Miracle was behind him now, back in the dining room.

Thompson hurried into the bedroom. A queen size bed lay unmade before him. A larger dresser stood off to his left, a closet to the right. A narrow line of windows ran along the top of the far wall, but no door that he could see, no balcony. If he had another instant, he might have tried hoisting himself through one of the windows, then trusting himself to whatever lay below. He heard Miracle, closer now, yammering. Thompson stepped into the closet, as far back as he could, hiding himself in the fragrant depths of the dead woman's clothes. The closet doors were slatted. Through those slats, in the instant before Miracle entered, Thompson saw his mistake. The balcony was directly across from him, outside an alcove in the opposite corner of the room. When he had first come in, the dresser had blocked it from his view. Now he could see plainly his avenue of escape. The sliding door was open, and he could see the rustling date palm and hear the sweet singing of some desert bird.

It was too late. Miracle stumbled in.

Thompson shook. His teeth chattered, as if from fever, and that sound alone, he feared, would draw Miracle to him.

The producer was more familiar with the room's layout than Thompson. He went directly to the alcove, then stepped onto the balcony. He peered down, studying the courtyard. He came back in, wild-eyed, and sat on the edge of the bed.

"He got away," Miracle said to himself, "the lousy son-of-bitch. Third-rate writer. Fucking hack."

Inside the closet, Thompson could not control his shaking. He breathed deep. A sob rose from the room—he felt it in his chest, it seemed, a horrible, ugly, gut-wrenching sob that put a terror in his heart. He sucked in his breath, doomed. Miracle did not move from the bed. The producer's shoulders were shaking, the sobbing went on, and Thompson realized it was the other man, not himself, from which the noise came, and the sound of his wailing bespoke how far things had drifted out of his control. *He needs my corpse,* Thompson thought. *With me alive, out in the world, it's too messy.* The man's story was unraveling in his head, and as it unraveled the tear in the seams became wider, and the details and the clutter came swarming up out of the abyss. Then the sobbing stopped. Miracle raised his head. He placed the gun into his mouth and pulled the trigger.

This time, the revolver's mechanism worked perfectly. The producer's body reeled backward, his skull exploded, and bits of red pulp and white bone flew into the paneling where Thompson stood watching.

Thompson stepped out of the closet. He thought about going down the balcony, but decided no, someone might have heard the gunshot. He did not want to be seen in the courtyard. So he went out of the apartment the way he had come, slipped out a side door. Outside, the flowers were whispering to one another, beasts were loose in the streets. The delirium had come. Thompson closed his eyes, and walked the best he could under that trembling line of palms.

THIRTY-FOUR

SEVERAL WEEKS LATER, ALBERTA stood on the steps outside the Hillcrest Arms, directing the moving men as they struggled the couch through the building door, then down the long hall to their apartment. Thompson stood watching his wife. She should be glum, but if she was, she wasn't going to let any one see it, not the neighbors, for certain, and not these moving men. She walked with a certain bounce. Her slacks were stylish, her blouse new, and she had given her hair a fresh rinse, not out of the bottle but hand-done at one of the professional joints, so she didn't look like just anyone.

Even so, something about her had changed. When it had happened, exactly, he wasn't sure. In the last few weeks, maybe, or maybe it had been happening all along—and he'd only just now noticed. For years, he had seen in her the seeds of the old woman she might someday become: the wrinkles; the dowager's hunch; the long blue veins emerging on her feet and hands. Always, though, it had been the woman she was at the moment who dominated: the girl being courted; the young wife; the taut, wiry female of middle age. Now, when he looked at her, he only occasionally saw those others. The young girl living at the edge of the cornfield had become an old woman in slacks, standing on a street corner in Los Angeles, smiling with a forced cheerfulness—and a deep embarrassment—at the young Mexican men who moved box after box of memorabilia into her too small apartment.

"How are you feeling?" She handed him a glass of water.

"Fine."

He took the glass, drinking it down as greedily as if he were one of the moving men, sweating in a sleeveless t-shirt.

"This apartment is cute," she said.

"It's a dump."

"The only trouble, it's too close to Musso's. The doctor said to keep away from temptation, you know, and. . ."

Thompson interrupted. "I'm not drinking anything stronger than this."

He handed her the empty water glass, and she walked away, back to the business of supervising. He hadn't had a drink since the day after he'd sneaked out of the hospital, but then he hadn't had much opportunity. After he'd left Michele Haze's apartment, he'd caught himself a taxi back to the Ardmore penthouse. His teeth had begun to rattle again in the back seat, more wildly, his bones to shake, and by the time he reached the door his whole body was in tremors. He knew it was no ordinary episode from the look Alberta gave him—and how quickly Doctor Rufus appeared. They'd taken him to the sanitarium, and there some white-coated doctors and a lisping nurse administered the nebutal and the anabuse and weaned him off the alcohol, but no matter the drugs, eventually it came down to himself alone, strapped to the bed, sweating and flailing while the phantasms uncoiled in the darkness and spoke to him in hissing tongues that he could feel wrapping around his body, licking, probing, crawling up his asshole, his intestines, then back out his mouth in hideous screams that shook the leeches from the ceiling and brought them tumbling onto his flesh, and these leeches had a new, strange language of their own.

During that time, the story of the Alameda Murders broke. It was all over the newspapers and the television and pieces of it filtered through to him in the sanitarium.

The speculation was wild and lurid—a third man at the murder scene, a connection to the underworld, a Hollywood serial killer on the loose—but how much of that was his own hallucination, the leeches whispering in the darkness, he didn't know, and it seemed to him as he came out of withdrawal that maybe all of it had been: the dead girl, the Okie, those memories of himself straggling along the hillside with a corpse over his shoulder. Either way, by the time he was discharged, the police had tied it all up in a neat little bow. Murder-suicide, the story went. Billy Miracle had killed Lombard when he backed off the deal. Apparently, Michele Haze had been ready to turn evidence against him. So he had killed her, too; then turned the gun on himself.

As for the girl in the hillside, she was not part of the equation. No one knew about her, no one cared.

Meanwhile, Alberta had used the money inside the envelope to pay for his treatment, and to buy a few more weeks at the Ardmore—because she was too busy going back and forth from the sanitarium to complete the move. Now, though, his stay was finished. And here they were.

•

Detective Mann showed up not long after they'd settled into the Hillcrest. A social call, he said, just to see how things were going. Alberta enjoyed the company. She liked the cop. He seemed earnest to her, clean cut and polite. Together they talked about a little town called Rabbit, not far from where she'd grown up.

"The cutest little town you ever seen."

"I know it.

"Full of picket fences."

"Houses with chimneys."

"Down home cooking."
"You bet."
"Indians live there."
"Colored too. Right alongside"
"Whites. Mexicans. Everyone in harmony."
"Not like it is here."
"No sir."
"No crime to speak of."
"That's a fact."
"Except, you know, there was a little something."
"It's the same way everywhere."
"The world's changed."
"Nothing like it used to be."
"A severed head, that's what it was. Belonged to a local banker. Found in the local creek."
"Oh, my God."
"My brother's a policeman on the local force, and they couldn't figure it out for the longest time. It just seemed like some random crime."
"Goes to show you."
"Yes, it does. Everyone in town, well they thought the banker had run off to California with his secretary—but it turns out bits and pieces of him and the woman, they were scattered all over town."
"You think it's the miscreants. But it's the upstanding ones."
"Wife did it. Jealous, I guess."
Alberta shook her head. "It's a darn shame, to see that happen in a place like Rabbit. Happens there, it can happen anywhere."
"Right in your own living room."
"Let's hope not," said Alberta. They laughed, and Alberta filled the detective's glass with more iced tea. They went on like that, gabbing away, until finally Mann got up to leave. Alberta said good-bye to him at the

door, and Thompson walked Mann out to his vehicle. It was parked on the same spot, more or less, where Thompson had first discovered the girl in the trunk of the Cadillac.

"Nice place you have," said Mann.

"No, it's not."

Mann looked at him. His eyes said go ahead, have it your way, and he leaned against the squad car. Thompson expected that now, alone, the cop would throw him a question or two about the Lombard murder, but instead there was just one of those long silences in which you could have heard the rise of the cicadas, if there had been cicadas, except of course there weren't any, not in this part of the country, just the sound of the transformer on the light pole overhead and the traffic rushing up Highland.

"So you still want my prints?"

"I been meaning to apologize about that. Reason I stopped by, I guess. But a man in my position, he has to examine every corner."

"How about my shoe size?"

Mann laughed. "Oh you mean that stray shoe. Well, it's a loose end, that's for sure, and if you want to come forward and claim it well, you can do that. And the wallet too. There's always stuff like that around a crime scene, with a logical explanation, harmless, innocent, but you don't know what that explanation is unless someone provides it."

Thompson looked away. This was the real reason Mann had come, he figured, because he still suspected those items belonged to Thompson, and wanted to know how they got to the scene. Thompson wasn't going to bite, not now.

"We did identify those prints, though," said Mann. "They belonged to Billy Miracle. We figured Michele

Haze may have been at the scene, too—or at least she knew about the murder."

"Why didn't she come forward?"

"She was afraid of Miracle, we figure. We had one of our men talking to her the day before she was killed. She was about to crack. A couple more days, and she would have given it up. Miracle must have figured the same."

Lieutenant Mann seem satisfied with this explanation. The official investigation was all but over, he said, there would be a final assembly of evidence, a report, a hearing, but the case would go down as solved. There were a couple curious details—odd blood smears, signs of scuffle at Haze's place, and that ancient revolver, unregistered, which Miracle must have picked up at a rummage sale, or some damned place.

"Not to change the subject," said Thompson, "but how about that guy on the street?"

"Which guy?"

"The one who tried to rob me."

"He'll turn up. Maybe not here, maybe not soon, but don't worry. Sometimes, a little piece of it just gets away from you. And because it's missing, you think it's bigger than it is, more important, and the whole world seems cock-eyed. But it's not cock-eyed. It's a just a little piece you don't understand."

"Sure," said Thompson

He noticed a flash in the cop's eyes, though, that let him know that maybe Mann didn't quite believe his own words. It was his job, sure, to wrap things up, put it all in some neat order and dismiss that which didn't fit. It's what people wanted from a cop. It wasn't too much different, when you got down to it, then what they wanted from a scientist, or a man of the cloth. Maybe Mann didn't believe it himself, maybe he'd spent too much time mucking in the blood and the mud to swallow his own nonsense, but it was his job to keep mucking, and to keep talking, too, like everything could be wrapped up and explained.

Himself, all he knew was that the Okie had stumbled on him, down there in front of Countdown Productions, by accident, by chance, maybe, but Alberta had beaten him away. The Okie was not the same man, precisely, that he had imagined for Billy Miracle, but they had intersected, the imaginary, the real, himself, though even in that moment of intersection, there was still a gap, an inexplicable space, a darkness that opened and kept opening.

And the Okie, he was still out there.

"In my profession, the imagination, it has to be disciplined. Otherwise it can lead you into dark corners," Mann gestured up the street at all the little houses, so peaceful under the cadmium lights. "Otherwise, all this, it goes to hell."

"I understand."

Lieutenant Mann put his hand on Thompson's shoulder, a friendly gesture it seemed, one man to the next, like they were two men of the same ilk, talking on the front porch back home, but he's pulling my leg, because underneath he's suspicious, he knows something has gotten loose from him (the dead girl, Thompson thought, buried on that hillside) and though he doesn't know what it is, he suspects me, because it's his job to remain on patrol after all, to be diligent as a man can be, to keep everything in its place.

"I'll be seeing you," the cop said.

"Sure."

Detective Orville Mann gave him his country boy smile. Then he tipped his hat, started his engine, and drove off into the twilight.

•

There was a story he had once yearned to write, but he had never done so. Fragments of the story were in everything he'd written but never in the right order, and never how he meant for them to be. He could blame people like Billy Miracle, or the publishing industry, or himself. He guessed, though, it was none of these.

The story had first occurred to him at the end of a long summer more than forty years before. He had been twenty-two years old, hitchhiking his way to Lincoln, Nebraska from the Texas oil fields, when he'd gotten stuck in a small town. Walking through the section of town with the old, substantial houses, he'd seen two young women on the front porch, sisters, he thought, because they looked something alike, even though one of them was beautiful and virginal, the other slack-jawed and hellish. He didn't know how he looked to them, like danger, maybe, something exciting about to happen, unshaven and coarse. He had given them a little wave. One of them had waved back, and the other had smiled—the kind of smile someone gives when they've been molesting you in their dreams—and he had the distinct impression he could have strolled up the walkway into the lives of those women. He went on ahead to the corner, then turned back, his heart filled with desire. The sisters still sat there, in the dull Texas heat, their dresses damp with sweat, their hair curling and moist, but he saw now a man walking up the steps, a sampler case in his hand, and heard the sisters giggling, and he knew then he'd lost his opportunity. So instead he had kept going, hitching off to his first year at college, until one day he stood on the porch of his true love, holding a bunch of flowers. And that was the story

Thompson had wanted to write, the story of that instant, of the young man standing on the porch with the flowers in his hand. The young man would be thinking about the girl inside, and he would remember those two sisters on that Texas porch, and meanwhile tiny no-see-um's would be crawling over his skin, biting him to beat Jesus. He would hold red flowers in his hand and when she opened the door her face would seem suddenly strange to him, beautiful, yes, but ugly too, and he would want suddenly both to smother her with kisses and to hurt her in some horrible way, while behind her the door opened into the darkness of the house with its antique furniture and walls hung with the pictures of dead relatives in ruffles and high-collared shirts, waiting for him to join them.

Thompson had wanted for the story to be tender and devastating, a void into which the reader would fall, experiencing the gap, the empty space, his desire had created within him, and he wanted the story to have within it unexpressed all the streets he would ever wander and his own past boyness too, and his sainted mother and his lost father, and the girl he had left behind, all somehow there without being there, without even having been mentioned. That was the story he had wanted to write once and would never write, he realized, because after all what was anybody but a stranger on the street, afraid for himself and what was inside him, and when you looked back it was always too late, as you caught the dark shadow of yourself—a traveling salesman, a returning father, a god without mercy—climbing the stairs you had been too afraid to climb, walking inside the soft door of your heart, murdering your dreams with his charms, his good looks, his unstoppable tongue.

THIRTY-FIVE

THE DAYS PASSED. He did not go back to the Aztec Hotel. He stayed away from Musso's. He did not drink (or he did not drink much), and he did not write. He thought sometimes of the girl buried by the freeway, and of the Oklahoman, and he sat in the small park across from the Hillcrest Arms and smoked his Pall Malls, taking the smoke deep into his lungs. There was something unfinished, he knew. Death was around the corner, but of course death always was. He should be hearing from his editor regarding the manuscript he'd written for Miracle. There was no movie deal anymore, even Countdown had lost interest, so full rights should be returning to him. Trouble was, everyone else had lost interest as well.

Alberta was still cool. She treated him with a politeness, a certain prim demeanor, as she moved about their shabby apartment. Even so, they found their own rhythm together. In the evening, the sun fell in long angles through the palms, and they would walk up the hill past all those houses with their gardenias and hydrangea and the birds of paradise growing on the other side of the picket fence. He'd see the women leaning over those fences, and hear the children playing, and the whole world would have that roseate glow. But there was always the other side too. Messages from the glowing tube in the corner, from the newspaper. Old women who had been knifed in their beds. Prowlers that crawled through windows. Bodies that washed ashore. Encyclopedia salesmen who came back in the middle of the night to steal children. And Thompson would lie beside Alberta thinking about those others. He felt at times she had to be thinking the same things as himself, but when he talked to her, she spoke in the same sort of Oklahoma platitudes she always spoke in. All we have is the here and now, honey, she would say. You know that. And there's no moon like the harvest moon. Because, the wind, well, it always blows hardest just before the corn is ripe. Things like that. But when he reached to touch her, she still rolled away in bed.

All this while, he heard nothing from his publisher. He decided to call Hector Sally, his editor. "I love it," Hector said, "there's just a few little changes I'd like to see. Give me a few days, and I'll get back to you."

Hector, though, did not call. When Thompson tried to contact him, the secretary said he was out. The next time, she told him he had left the firm. The new editor couldn't find the manuscript.

"I love your writing, Jim," said the new man. "I'm a big son-of-bitch fan, but I'm afraid it isn't here."

"What do you mean, it isn't there?"

"I am afraid it's lost."

"Lost? It's my only copy."

"No carbon?"

"I've got fragments. Bits and pieces. But not the whole manuscript."

"That's a shame—but maybe you could fill in the gaps somehow. Of course, your time is valuable, I know, and our list for next fall, it's pretty full. No guarantees, you understand."

Thompson realized he was being given the kiss off. For some reason, he did not care. In a way, it was liberating. He didn't have to worry about it anymore.

He told Alberta.

"I'm finished," he said. "I give up."

She brought him some collard greens she had made, and sat down pleasantly at the table beside him. She reached out and touched his thigh. He could smell that old cornfield now, as if it were right outside the window.

"Should we go do something this evening?" she asked.

"That would be nice."

They went out for malts at a drive-in diner, and sat in the car. Girls in skates brought the food, and kids hung around running combs through their greased-up hair, as if they all lived in an earlier decade.

"Let's take a drive," she said.

They drove for hours. Down to Bunker Hill, then out to Santa Monica, along the Palisades, and back up through the Malibu canyons into the city, but at the end of it he was still not quite ready to go home, and neither was she, and so they drove up Whitley Terrace, and he pulled down the gravel road overlooking the freeway. Alberta wanted to get out and look at the Whitely Cross, and the lights of the cars rushing down towards Hollywood, so that's what they did. After a while, they wandered over to the other side of the hill. Thompson could see the spot where the girl lay buried, he was pretty sure, down slope, below the eucalyptus, just off the trail. Weeds had started to grow over the site, and Thompson knew now it would be a long time before anyone found her body.

"I'm sorry," he told Alberta.

"Why?"

"For everything. The rummy apartment. The crummy smell in the upholstery."

She didn't say anything.

"I can't give it up."

"What?"

"None of it."

"What do you mean?"

"I was down on the Boulevard yesterday. I had a drink."

"I know," she said.

"I have an evil in my heart."

"I know that, too."

She leaned against him—accepting him again, as she had done in the past, the old circle spinning around, so it was her fingers reaching for his—then she kissed him, hard, and he felt a thrill within him, the old erection erecting, and she put a hand on his belt, and he looked her in the eyes, and there was a gleam that frightened him, and he remembered that hungry girl she had been, and how much she had surprised him with her ferocity.

Meanwhile, there was that other girl down there, still in her grave. Whatever her name was. The innocent one.

"What did you do with Lucille?" she asked.

"What do you mean?"

"You saw her when she was here?"

"No."

"You wanted to see her?"

He hesitated. "No," he said.

She did not believe him. She was jealous, he guessed. Anyway he could see a gleam in her eyes, a hunger, and a little bit of anger too. They went home then, and though her anger was still there, she rolled sideways in the bed, pulling him towards her, and he felt the hot flush of the blood rising to his skin. He pulled up her nightgown, feeling her nakedness there, her stomach against his, and her breath heavy in his ear. As he touched her, he thought about the book he had written and how he might salvage what was left. He would call his editor. As he caressed her, in his mind, he had already made the call. He could hear his editor's voice.

"What's your idea?"

"I'll use pieces of the old book, the parts I have left. And I'll write another book around it. About an old man, in Los Angeles. He's a crime writer, trying to write a story about his life. Except he doesn't realize it until the last few pages, and by that time, well, he's become character in his own book." And the more he thought about it, the more the lines dissolved, between the living and the imagined, between those who called and those who were summoned. Because while it might be Lieutenant Mann's job to separate good from evil, his own was quite the opposite.

"Sounds great, Jim." It was a flat voice, full of irony. "What will you call it?"

Thompson hesitated. "Same title. *Manifesto for the Dead.*"

"Brilliant."

Even as he spoke, he knew the new man was only humoring him, betting the manuscript would not be finished. That old Jim Thompson would kick the bucket, or otherwise disappear. And as he turned again towards his wife—both passionately involved and distant, separated from her even as he felt his erection growing and felt too the wild thrill of her flesh, as if their whole life had been building towards this instant—Thompson figured maybe the editor was correct. Maybe he would not write the book. He would not live. He felt himself already becoming a figure in someone else's story, drifting over the border. If it wasn't the Oklahoman who got him, it would be something else. A stroke. Congestive heart failure. A stranger slipping through the window and taking him in the middle of the night. He was joining that other world. Maybe he already had. Maybe he lay on his deathbed and this moment, now, was pure imagination. He was a figure in someone else's dream. It didn't matter. He was on top of Alberta, she was clasping him to her. He couldn't help himself. He loved the moment of descent, he could not resist, and neither could his wife. There was fierceness in the air. Lust. Desire. Her body was skeletal, hideous, beautiful in its ugliness, homely and horrifying. He kept after her, and she was pulling him down into her, and he felt his heart pounding too heavily, the blood rushing to the head, and she was whispering in his ear, incomprehensible words, beckoning him closer, and that's what he was doing, plunging into that forbidden darkness. Then more darkness, and figures moving there, and somewhere a border that once you crossed you did not come back. He knew before long he would slip over that border, into that blackness, and he would leave behind his own calligraphy, a dark looking-glass, for those who would follow him down.